ON THE LINE

An Out of Line Novel

JEN MCLAUGHLIN

NEW YORK TIMES BESTSELLING AUTHOR
JEN MCLAUGHLIN

ON THE LINE

AN OUT OF LINE NOVEL

Cover Designed by: ProBook Premade Book Covers

Interior Design and Formatting by:

eBook ISBN: **978-0-9907819-9-8**

Print ISBN: **978-0-9907819-8-1**

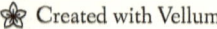 Created with Vellum

This one goes out to my grandfather, who suffered from dementia in his last year. There isn't a day we don't miss you, Pee-Paw.

ONE

Sarah

———

The bloated, distorted features of the woman's face were almost unrecognizable. The sun shone off the waters of the bay, casting a cheery glow upon the otherwise dismal scene. Birds sang in the distance as a seagull sat on the hot sand staring at me, almost as if it knew that I felt as unqualified for this job as the man who had drove drunk and put this woman into the bay two nights ago.

Swallowing hard, I glanced at the picture in my hand, then back at the pale, swollen face that had already become a meal for some hungry fish. Though it was almost impossible to distinguish one feature from the next, I had no doubt as to who lay on the shore. "It's definitely Mary Hendricks."

Behind me, my male partner (who took the role of overbearing alpha male to a whole new level) shifted his weight onto the balls of his feet and scoffed. "Just like that?"

"Just like that," I said, tilting my head back to stare at the man who Captain had paired me with—more than likely, on purpose. Just to torture me. "Is there a problem, Rollins?"

"Yeah. I don't know how you did it in North Carolina, but in California? We usually wait for DNA or dental records to state who our victims are."

If I heard that phrase one more time, I was going to explode.

Ever since I'd come back to California, everyone had been throwing my abrupt departure for college in my face, as if it had been a bad thing to spread my wings and go elsewhere for a few years. Everyone might not know it, but I had a pretty good reason for doing so, and if anyone should know that reason...it was my partner. I'd had a damn good reason for fleeing, and he knew it. Just like I had a damn good reason for coming back, after all this time.

"We did the same in North Carolina, but in this case?" I gestured at the victim's arm, pointing at the tattoo that said *Girl Power*. "I was with Mary when she got this tattoo, as well as the one below it." This time, I pointed at the tattoo that had *MLH* in fancy scrawl. "Which literally has her initials on it, so, yeah, I'm going to go ahead and say that this is Mary Hendricks."

Rollins flexed his jaw, staring down at me. "Still, no official word will be spread until we get the results back from forensics."

"Obviously," I said dryly, standing and swiping my free hand on my pencil skirt. I'd worn a light khaki colored one today, along with a checkered blouse. Every day when I dressed, I spent way too long agonizing over what outfit would represent the woman I was now—strong, empowered, independent, responsible—as opposed to the girl I'd been—irresponsible, reckless, wild. The girl who had gotten her heart broken, and run away instead of facing the pain.

I wasn't that girl anymore.

Too bad no one else could see that.

Rollins gestured to CSI. "It's all yours."

"Thank you," I said, smiling at them.

None of them met my eyes. Typical.

Rollins started toward our waiting car without waiting for me. I followed him, studying his broad biceps and even broader arms. Once upon a time, I'd clung to those shoulders as he kissed me sweetly and told me he loved me, but that had been years ago, when I'd been another person. I wasn't that naive girl anymore, no matter what anyone else thought.

Sliding into the passenger seat, I opened the file I'd placed on hold and set the photos inside it, scribbling my thoughts down on the legal pad. As I wrote, I could feel Rollins' eyes on me.

"What?" I asked, not lifting my head.

"Why are you writing on paper? You'll just have to do it again later."

"Because I don't want to forget anything."

He started the car, shaking his head. "Okay."

I bit my tongue, refusing to rise to the bait. He'd been trying to get under my skin from the moment we'd been assigned as partners, and I wasn't about to let him succeed. "I remember things better when they're fresh in my mind."

"As I recall it, you never forget anything."

The sarcasm in his tone was impossible to miss. "I don't forget things that are important to me, no."

"So, your job isn't?" he immediately shot back.

"I didn't say that." I set the pen down and looked at him. "Don't put words in my mouth, Rollins."

He rolled his eyes at my use of his last name. In my opinion, just because we'd seen each other naked years ago didn't mean we needed to be on a first name basis on the job. Not to mention that had been a lifetime ago, and I'd never make that mistake again. "As I recall, you hate it when I do that, too."

"Then don't do it."

He shrugged. "What would be the fun in that?"

The sun gleamed through his driver's window, shining off his blond hair and almost blinding me. His jaw was hard, chiseled from stone, and he pressed his mouth into a tight line, like he usually did around me. His green eyes currently hid behind shades, but more than likely he'd narrowed them on the road as he gripped the steering wheel so tight his knuckles showed white. He wore a black suit with a white button up shirt and a sensible tie, like usual.

It annoyed me how handsome he was, mostly because *he* annoyed *me* so much.

"Do you get off on picking on me?" I asked, unable to help myself.

So much for not taking the bait.

His lips quirked into a smirk. "You know what gets me off."

"No, I don't."

The smirk widened. "Oh, right. That's one of the reasons we broke up—you never gave a damn about what I wanted out of life."

And just like that, I lost my cool. *Damn him.* "As I recall it, we broke up because you—" I cut myself off. Not doing this. Not fighting with my ex. *Nope.*

He slammed his breaks at the red light, swiveling to face me with flared nostrils. "Because I did *what*, Sarah?"

"Light's green," I said dryly, arching my brows, refusing to answer him.

He knew what he did. He just thought *I* didn't know.

He muttered a few choice words and stepped on the gas, his knuckles even tighter on the wheel than before. It was a miracle it didn't break under pressure. "This is a horrible idea."

"What is?"

"Us, together again." He glanced at me out of the corner of his eye. "You need to ask for reassignment."

I rolled my eyes. "*You* can ask for reassignment."

"Why me?" he demanded.

"Why *me*?"

He pulled into the parking spot and slammed the car into park. "Because you're the one who waltzed back into town, thrusting yourself into my life uninvited, and—"

"I didn't thrust into anything of yours."

Yanking his keys out of the ignition, he pressed his lips together. "I know. I remember that, too."

I closed my eyes and counted to three. It did nothing to calm me down. "I swear to God, Rollins—"

"What?" He blinked at me innocently. "Too much?"

I glared at him, saying nothing.

"There's an easy fix to this."

Gripping the door handle, I unbuckled and hugged my file to my chest. My heart beat hard against it, faster than usual. Probably because of *him*, which only made me angrier. He took his shades off, and the force of his eyes locking on mine almost made me hold my breath. *Almost*.

"Oh yeah? And what's that?" I managed to ask.

"Do what you do best. Give up and walk away." With that, he took his own advice, opened his car door, and walked away.

If only it was as easy for me to do.

TWO

Ben

———

"*I*t isn't working," I said slowly, staring at my empty beer with my jaw clenched. Ever since Sarah had come back into town, my jaw had been in a permanent state of tension. Now I spent most of my nights tossing and turning, torn between fantasizing about her soft lips and even softer hair, and wanting to scream at her to get the hell out of my town like she had ten years ago.

"Well, duh," my best friend, and old partner, said. "I could have told you that." He paused, tapping his chin. "Oh, wait, I *did* tell you that."

"I told Captain the same thing, but he said that he was pissed the commissioner made him take her on, so the best way to scare her off was to pair her with the only person she hates more than him."

Hernandez snorted. "You."

"Yep, me."

"Yeah, well, your dad's an asshole," Hernandez said, grinning.

"Yep."

"And so are you," my best friend added helpfully.

I shrugged. "Probably." After a moment of silence, I added, "You know, she has yet to use my real name. Insists on calling me Rollins."

"We all use last names," Hernandez said, frowning. "Hell, no one uses my real name."

One of our friends, and Hernandez's old combat buddy, Finn Coram, slid into the seat next to us. He didn't drink, so he was sipping on a coke instead of a beer. "Carrie does."

"Carrie's the only exception," Hernandez said. "How is she, anyway? And how's Cory?"

"Great, and great. He's walking," Finn said, grinning with pride. Carrie and Finn had been married for almost ten years, and were quite happily the parents of two children, one of which was a little over a year old. "And adorable as hell."

"Of course," Hernandez agreed.

I nodded, too. "Obviously."

"So what are we talking about?" Finn asked, settling in.

"Ben's ex, and how she calls him Rollins instead of Ben."

Finn frowned. "Don't all cops do that?"

"Yeah, but we haven't all fucked one another, have we?" I shot back.

"I don't know," Hernandez said his lip quirking up in a smile. "There was that one time where we woke up in that bed—"

"Shut the fuck up," I growled.

Hernandez laughed, but did indeed shut the fuck up.

Finn arched a brow. "Man, I'd love to hear that story."

"Did she ever tell you why she ran?" Hernandez asked.

"No, and I don't give a damn," I muttered. It was a lie. I gave a damn. How could I not? We'd been happy, and the high school's IT couple. Everyone envied us, hated us, or wanted to be us. Then one day she just decides to stop talking to me, asks for space, and then moves to North Carolina for college after telling me she was done, with tears streaming down her face? Yeah. I cared. "It was forever ago."

"You totally sound like a guy who doesn't give a damn," Hernandez said dryly. His dark brown hair was as perfectly combed back as always, and his deep brown eyes were shining with amusement—again, as always. Despite his time in the Marines, and all the shit he'd seen overseas, there was nothing that my best friend couldn't find humor in... including my current plight of being partnered with the one woman who had managed to break my heart.

I flipped him off.

Finn pointed at me, staring me down. "You totally want to know. Don't bullshit us."

I said nothing.

The bartender came over with our refills. Thank God. "Thanks, Molly."

She winked at me. "Anything for you, Officer."

"Detective," Hernandez supplied helpfully.

She shrugged. "Whatever."

Hernandez opened his mouth, losing his laughing-at-the-world look, but Finn elbowed him. "Let her be," he whispered.

"She just said—" Hernandez started, gesturing at her angrily.

"I know." I picked up my beer. "Let it go."

"Whatever," he echoed. Hernandez huffily picked up his Guinness, scowling at her back. "You're not allowed to fuck her."

I choked on my beer, coughing.

Finn burst into laughter. Half the feminine eyes turned

toward him with interest, but they were wasting their time. Finn only had eyes for his wife. "Jesus, Hernandez."

"What?" Hernandez said innocently. "She's been eyeing him for years. It's no secret she wants it."

"Not interested," I muttered.

In fact, the only woman I'd been interested in lately was my reluctant partner. Too bad I'd already had her once, and she'd broken my heart. *Why* had she come back to Somerton? It was bad enough she'd run away in the first place, but then she had the gall to pretend it had been my fault that she decided she didn't love me anymore? One day, we'd been happy and planning to attend college together. The next, she was asking for space, and then telling me she'd changed her mind, accepted a spot at Duke, and then she was gone.

Just like that.

She hadn't even told me why.

Four years of dating, dreams, and plans in high school— and I didn't even get a fucking explanation? And yet *I* was the bad guy?

"You have a thing for her still." Finn said, breaking the silence. He gestured at Hernandez. "Just like this one and Marie."

"Fuck you," Hernandez said, scowling, losing his jovial air for the first time that night. "I never had a thing for her, and still don't."

"Yeah, okay," Finn agreed, rolling his bright blue eyes.

"She has to go," I cut in, interrupting what would surely turn into a fight I'd already heard a million times before. It was an ongoing argument between the two friends, and had been for as long as I'd known them.

Finn shrugged. "So get rid of her."

"I can't." I ran my hand down my face. "I told her to

request a transfer. She refused."

Finn lifted a brow. "Then you ask for one."

"I did." I frowned. "Dad said no."

You know, I didn't even know why she decided to become a cop. Last I'd spoken to her, she'd been planning on a career in Psychology. Then, all of a sudden, she's back and she's my partner? How did that even happen? Why'd she change her mind? Oh. Right. That's what she did. Changed her mind without warning.

It was her thing.

Hernandez set his beer down, his eyes shining in that way that could only hint that he was about to come up with a devious plan. Last time I had seen that look, the local high school mascot had ended up on the school roof—and no, we hadn't been in high school at the time. Captain had been *pissed*. "So, make it happen."

"How?" I asked cautiously.

"You two have history."

I rolled my eyes. "No shit, Sherlock."

"Well, use it."

"That's fucked up, man," Finn said, whistling through his teeth.

I stiffened, catching on to what he was saying. "No way."

"Why not?" Hernandez shifted closer, his eyes shining.

"Because he's not an asshole," Finn answered for me.

I pointed at Finn. "What he said."

"If Captain finds out you two are fucking, which goes against his policy, then he'll have no choice but to reassign one—or both—of you. Or he may even terminate her employment." Hernandez shrugged. "Maybe I'll even get my partner back."

Finn shook his head, clearly not liking this plan.

Neither did I. "I do miss being your partner... But still, I can't do it. Not even to her."

"Suit yourself," Hernandez said.

"Besides, she wouldn't even want to. She seems to blame me for whatever led to her leaving all those years ago —which makes no sense."

Hernandez snorted. "Not at all. She's the one who screwed you over—not the other way around. She deserves whatever you throw at her, if you ask me."

"She didn't screw me over." I frowned at my beer. "She just left. People leave."

Finn shook his head, surveying the crowd around them. He never chilled and just enjoyed his time. He was always on alert. Always watching. Guess that came with being the son-in-law of a high-profile presidential candidate, though. "Not like that."

"Exactly." Hernandez picked up his beer. "Did you tell her you cried after she left you?"

I snorted. "No."

"Maybe you should," Hernandez said.

"Yeah. That'll scare her off," Finn added.

This time, *he* earned my middle finger.

"I'm telling you, my plan is flawless. Not only does it allow for a little bit of revenge, but it also gets rid of her. Because we all know what'll happen if you two get back together again," Hernandez said cryptically.

I lifted a brow. "Besides us getting reassigned?"

"Yep."

Sighing, I took the bait against my better judgement and asked, "What?"

"Well..." Hernandez grinned. "She'll run off on you again, of course."

"Fuck you," I growled.

THREE

Sarah

I walked into my kitchen, rubbing the back of my neck, grimacing at all the knots that had developed since coming back to this town. Since my return, everyone had tried to belittle me, and make me quit. So I'd had to work twice as hard as my coworkers to prove myself... including my partner.

Part of that was because I was a woman, but most of it was because I was who I was—the girl who had left, and then came back to town with my tail between my legs. If it had been up to me, I never would have set foot back here again, but it hadn't been up to me, had it? Plastering a smile on my face, I called out, "Grace?"

Grace came out, wearing blue scrubs today, and a weary look on her face. "Hey. You're back."

"Yes, sorry I'm late, I had to work on a case." I set my purse on the table next to the millions of prescription bottles. "How is she today?"

"Not too great," Grace said slowly. We'd been friends, once upon a time, so when it came time to find a full-time nurse for my mom, it only made sense to go to a familiar

12

face. It had to be someone I could trust, and privacy was a number one priority for me. No one needed to know about my mom's health issues. I didn't need even more people doubting my commitment to the job, and my abilities to focus when on the case. They'd use anything to get rid of me.

Of that I had no doubt.

Especially my partner.

"Was she upset?" I asked.

"For a little while. After the sun went down, like usual." She sat down, letting out a long sigh. "With dementia, that's normal. They call it Sundowners Syndrome. Her disease is progressing, and unfortunately it'll probably be downhill from here, especially in the evenings." She paused. "I'm not going to sugarcoat it for you. This isn't going to be easy."

I swallowed hard. "It never is, is it?"

Grace shook her head. "I'm willing to be here full time, you know that, but ultimately, you might end up having to place her in a home. Sometimes that's the safest option for dementia patients who require around the clock care."

"No." I rubbed my temples, my heart wrenching at the idea of putting my mother in a facility. "I can do this. I can take care of her."

Grace nodded, reaching down to her bag and pulling out a stack of papers and catalogs. "Okay. Here's the stuff I was telling you about. Also, I included some catalogs. It's a good idea to change the lock system so she can't get out in the middle of the night while you're sleeping."

I swallowed past my aching throat. This was too much. The idea of my mother slipping outside unattended while I slept... God, could I do this? Could I oversee my mom's safety? Could I...? *Yes*, I could. I had no choice. This was my *mother*. One way or another, I'd do what I had to do.

"Th-Thank you," I managed to say.

Grace eyed me sympathetically, reaching out and squeezing my hand. "I'm here for you, anything you need, I'm here. Did you tell Ben about your mom?"

"No, absolutely not." I pulled free. "No one can know what I'm dealing with. Knowing them, they'd somehow use it against me, and try to say I'm unfit for the job. Captain didn't even want to let me in, and my old boss had to pull some major favors for me. They'd jump at any opportunity to get rid of me, so I'm not giving them one. What happens in my house is my business, and only mine."

Grace shook her head. "I don't think Ben would do that. He's a good guy."

Yeah, so good he'd cheated on me, and then acted like I'd been the bad guy for running away because it hurt too much. "Yeah. He's great." I swallowed, studying Grace's flushed cheeks. "Did you two... Are you two...?"

"No." Grace shook her head. "We had a thing, one night, years ago, but he's always been nothing but kind to me. I think he'd surprise you, despite your past."

I shrugged, not liking the idea of Ben's hands on my former best friend. We might have ended things years ago, but it still hurt. Out of all the girls in Somerton, he'd had to go after *Grace*? "Maybe, maybe not. I won't be finding out."

I didn't trust Ben, not one little bit.

Grace stood, smiling and tucking her hair behind her ears. "Well, I guess I'll be going home now. Seven in the morning again?"

"Yes, please." I stood too. "Thank you."

"Anytime."

Grace left, closing the door behind her. I took a second to cover my face, take a shuddering breath, and feel sorry for myself—and my mom.

But that was all I gave myself. One second.

Then I put my big girl panties on, as my mother used to always say, and made my way into the back of the house, to my mom's room. "Good evening."

As I entered, I braced myself for the moment when my mother looked at me...and had no clue who I was. My mom, whose brown eyes had once held warmth and pride whenever they looked at me, were flat and lifeless as they studied me now. There was no warmth. No pride. Just confusion. "Are you the night nurse tonight?"

"Yes. I'm the night nurse. Are you hungry?"

She hesitated. "A little."

"What would you like?"

Mom frowned. "Pudding. I'd like chocolate pudding, with rainbow sprinkles. Don't be cheap with the sprinkles, they're my favorite part."

"I know," I managed to say, keeping the smile on my face despite the looming tears. "I'll give you *extra* extra sprinkles. I promise."

"And check on my baby. I heard her crying earlier."

Swallowing past the pain, I nodded, going along with my mother's words even though it hurt more than I could ever possibly describe. In my mom's world, I was still a baby, and she was still a young single mother fighting to make ends meet. I'd never known just how much she struggled until she'd forgotten who I was, and talked to me as a colleague, instead of her child. A tear escaped down my cheek, but I angrily swiped it away. "I'll check on Sarah, don't worry."

Mom relaxed against the pillow. "Good. That child... Honestly, she never stops crying. The girl's going to have to toughen up."

"I've got her," I promised, biting down on my lip so hard it hurt. "I'll tell her."

As I walked out, I swiped the tears off my cheeks and straightened my spine, mentally telling myself to knock it off, and pull it together. I missed my mom. Missed having her arms around me, hugging me, and telling me everything would be all right, because *God*, I needed someone to tell me everything was going to be okay right about now.

FOUR

Ben
_____

*T*he next morning, I walked over to Sarah's desk slowly, studying her as I drew closer. She typed furiously, her forehead slightly scrunched in concentration like she used to do back in high school. She was biting her bottom lip as her fingers flew over the keys. Her face looked a little pale today, and she had bags under her eyes, as if she hadn't slept well the night before.

Why hadn't she slept well the night before?

Had she been with someone? That, of course, was none of my damn business. Not anymore. And yet...I couldn't stop the jealousy rolling in my gut at the thought of some other man keeping her up late at night. Once upon a time, that had been my job. I'd been good at it.

That hadn't stopped her from leaving, though.

Her long brown hair was pulled back in a sensible bun today, but I knew from memory how soft it felt against my fingers, and how long it was when she let it fall down her back in thick waves. Her medium skin was softer than the finest silks, and her dark brown eyes, when they weren't glaring at me in frustration, would shine with life and thought. She might only be five-foot-two, but when she was pissed at me (which was often) she gave off the appearance of a much larger woman. I knew that from experience, too.

All too well.

As if she sensed my approach, she lifted her head. She did indeed have bags under her eyes, so I'd been right about the not sleeping part. "Late night?" I asked dryly, unable to stop myself.

She frowned. "Why would you ask me that?"

"Bags." I pointed at my eyes. "For days."

She lifted her fingers to her cheeks, flushing slightly. "Oh."

"Go out dancing?"

Her lush red lips pressed into a thin line. "No. I didn't go out dancing."

"Oh. A hot date?"

She slammed her glasses down. "*No.*"

"Why are you so angry?" I asked, holding my hands up in surrender. "As I recall, you love hitting the clubs, dancing with strangers, and getting—"

"That was when I was a teenager," she snapped, setting her hands into her lap to keep me from seeing how irritated she was. It didn't work. I saw. I always saw...and I knew all her tricks. "I haven't gone dancing in a club since my second year at college."

I lifted a brow, shifting the file I was holding to my left hand. "Why not?"

"Because—" She stopped talking, narrowing her eyes. Ah, there it was. The cool disdain she always showed me. "Do you need something, Rollins?"

If she called me Rollins one more time... I slapped the file on my open palm, forcing a smile I didn't feel. "Yeah, we have a case. Let's go."

"But I'm still working on—"

"And now you're working on another." I challenged her with my stare. "Unless you can't handle that? Are you incapable of multitasking?"

Stiffening, she stood. She wore a plaid shirt tucked into a pair of black trousers, with a black blazer on top. It was professional. Prim. Proper. I still couldn't take my eyes off her. "I am perfectly capable."

"Well, then?" I said cockily, gesturing for the door.

Saying nothing, she brushed past me, her arm barely touching my abs—yet I felt it. *Fuck*, did I feel it. Being around her was torturous. It might have been years since she'd been mine, but I'd never gotten over her. Not completely. For me, it had always been her.

Sometimes I feared it would always *be* her, too.

I followed her, doing my best to keep my gaze transfixed on the back of her head, instead of dipping down to her swinging hips. She'd always had a way of walking that kind of made it look like she floated, and the gracefulness with which she moved defied gravity itself. And the way those pants hugged her ass? A gift from heaven itself.

Halfway toward the door, someone grabbed my arm. Hernandez stepped in front of me. "Dude."

"What?" I asked, blinking, snapping out of it.

"I was just kidding, you know."

Now I was really confused—and behind. Sarah was already outside. I shifted my feet restlessly. "About what?"

"Seducing her." Hernandez glanced over his shoulder and shuffled closer. "I didn't mean it. That's playing dirty, man."

I blinked again. "I'm not seducing her."

"So, you're just staring at her like you're starving and she's a steak for fun, then?"

Shit. Had I been staring?

"*Ohhhh.*" Hernandez nodded, eyeing me up. "Oh. I see."

"You see what?" I asked between clenched teeth.

"Why this isn't going to work." He stepped back, rubbing his jaw. "You still have a thing for her."

"I do *not*."

Hernandez snorted. "Yeah. Okay."

The door opened, and Sarah stuck her head in, her Ray Bans lowered on her nose. "Rollins? You coming?"

Hernandez snorted.

I elbowed him. "Yeah, I'm coming."

"No, you're not," Hernandez muttered.

I walked away, ignoring my best friend. As I approached, Sarah held the door for me politely. For some reason, this pissed me off even more. "Thanks," I said under my breath.

She eyed me. "What's wrong?"

"Nothing."

She fell into step beside me. "If you say so."

"I do." I took the keys out to my car, unlocking it. "I'm driving."

Sighing, she walked to the passenger side of my black Charger. "You always drive."

"I saw your driving record."

Her cheeks flushed as she slid into her seat. "You did a background check on me?"

"Of course I did. I always do when I get a new partner." I started the car and slid my shades into place. "Want to tell me about what happened in that club in North Carolina?"

Her cheeks went even redder. "Nope."

"Fine." I shrugged. "It won't beat what I've imagined anyway, I'm sure."

Her jaw fell. "How could you possibly think something dirty happened that night? You read the report."

"It's my specialty to find dirtiness in everything."

"It was nothing like *that*," I snapped.

"Then what was it?"

"It was none of your damn business," she said immediately, smiling sweetly at me.

How did she manage to look like an angel, with the promise of death blazing in her eyes? "Suit yourself."

"Want to tell me about December two years ago?" she shot back.

I backed out of my spot. "Nope."

"That's what I thought."

I gritted my teeth and pulled out onto the road. "Actually, you know what? I will. I went to the bar, and there was an asshole there picking on a group of out of towners, throwing racial slurs left and right. So I stood up, asked him to leave, and he refused. When he refused?" I shrugged a shoulder. "I showed him the way out personally."

"With your fist," she said softly.

"Among other things."

She nodded, staring out the window. "Good."

"I told you mine, now you tell me yours."

Sighing, she traced an invisible path on the door. "I was seeing a guy who wasn't so nice. He got mad at me for talking to my study partner—a cute guy—and punched him. When I tried to stop him, he dragged me away and hit me—"

I growled under my breath.

"And broke my nose." She touched her nose as if it was visible. It wasn't. "He threatened to kill me if I told them he did it, so I told them I got punched by some girl in a bar fight over a guy."

I swallowed hard. "Did he hit you before that?"

"He…" She stiffened. "Does it matter?"

"Sarah…"

Sighing, she fidgeted with her seat belt. "It's done. He's gone. It doesn't matter."

Son of a bitch. "Just tell me one thing. Is he in jail?"

She lifted a shoulder. "He was when I left."

He better be in jail. If he wasn't, I might have to pay him a visit. Then again…maybe it would be better if he wasn't. Clearly, the man needed someone to remind him how to properly treat a lady.

And I knew just the way to do so.

FIVE

Sarah

I shouldn't have told him that. It was none of his business what kind of bad life choices I had made after I'd left Somerset. Just like it was none of mine what had happened that night he'd gotten himself locked up for a bar fight. But when he'd told me about his secret, it had just seemed right to do the same.

Sighing, I eyed him carefully. He stared out the windshield, focused on the road, and it took all my willpower not to stare at him. His jaw was so hard and his stubble begged for my fingers to touch it. To see if it was as crisp as I imagined. My fingers twitched in my lap, but instead of finding out, I picked up the file he'd set between us instead.

As I opened it, he spoke.

"Domestic violence call."

My heart sank, and my palms started to sweat. Out of all the cases to get...

No. I could do this.

"The husband has a history of abuse, and no one has heard from the wife for three days. No show for work. No phone calls. No emails. Nothing." Ben flexed his jaw, his grip on the steering wheel tight. "Her mother called it in, concerned he might have hurt her again."

No one had known what Vinnie had done to me. He'd scared me into silence, and had threatened to take everything away from me if I opened my mouth. I'd believed him for too long.

Pushing my own thoughts aside, I frowned at the file. There were countless reports of abuse, and arrests. I glanced at the family profile, relieved to see there were no children in the home. "We don't usually make house calls. Why this one?"

He didn't bother to deny this was a special exception. "Captain is friends with the mother."

"Ah." I glanced at the name, recognizing it instantly. "Shit. Liz?"

He nodded, his jaw still tight.

I remembered Liz. She'd always been quiet, shy. Even back then, she'd cowered behind her football playing boyfriend, never speaking out of turn. Guess they'd stayed together, and gotten married. Too bad she hadn't left town for college, and tried to find a guy who wouldn't treat her horribly. "She *married* him?"

He nodded again.

I stared at the reports of abuse, feeling sick to my stomach. "She should've left town. Tried to find somewhere else where she wasn't stuck standing behind him, keeping his shadow company."

He looked at me slowly, his shades hiding his eyes. "Not everyone can just pack up their shit and go, Sarah. Sometimes, people stay. Sometimes they don't have a choice. You're lucky that you were able to leave your situation, but not everyone can."

Tensing, I stared down at the file. This wasn't about me.

24

It was about a woman who may or may not be okay, all because of an asshole who didn't know how to treat a woman right.

We were silent the rest of the ride.

After a few minutes, he pulled up to a one-story, brick home. Someone mowed the lawn recently. Pruned flowers filled the flowerbeds, and the porch held no clutter. Just some wicker furniture, a table, and a wind chime adorned it. Everything had been carefully arranged, pristine. Too pristine.

Ben frowned. "I don't like this. I have a bad feeling."

I swallowed hard. A shiver went up my spine. "Me too."

"Approach with caution," he said, opening his door.

I did the same, my hand on my Glock. "Together, or do you want to go around the back?"

"Together." He surveyed the house, frowning. "I don't want one of us being taken off guard."

I nodded, not speaking, watching his back and surveying the surrounding trees. Nothing moved. Nothing made a sound. It was quiet. *Too* quiet. The hairs rose on the back of my neck, and I crept closer to Ben. I might not like it, but he was my partner, and I'd be damned if something happened to him on my watch. As he went up the stairs to the porch, I noticed something I hadn't seen from the driveway.

A stack of mail on the table beside the door.

Packages, flyers, letters. *All untouched.*

The hair on the back of my neck rose higher, and I stopped walking. "Ben."

He glanced back at me, his eyes slightly wide. It wasn't until his wide eyes registered with mine that I realized I'd used his first name for the first time since we'd been paired up. "Yeah?"

"Hold up." I stepped closer. "We should call for back up."

"Why?" he asked, frowning.

"I have a feeling. A bad one."

I half expected him to make fun of me, or say something about how around here, they didn't work on *feelings*, but facts. Instead, he surprised me. "I do, too. Unfortunately, I don't think we need back up."

"But..." I blinked. "What do you mean?"

"Breathe deeply."

Frowning, I did as told. Roses. Grass. Trees. And then... Oh, God. And then, I smelled it. "*No.*"

"Shit," Ben muttered, walking closer and approaching the door carefully. "Think it's one of them, or both?"

"I don't know," I said, breathing through my mouth, instead of my nose, but it didn't help. Now that I'd smelled it, there was no *un*smelling it. "Should we call for backup just in case?"

He shook his head, his gaze on the front window as he removed his hand from the butt of his pistol. "No need."

Even though it was pretty much the last thing I wanted to do, I approached, looking through the window, also. There they were—two bodies in varying stages of decomposition. There was no mistaking the fact that they were both dead. *Very* dead. Liz lay to the left of her husband, her shirt covered with dried up blood on her chest. There was a line of blood across the floor, as if she might have tried to crawl away but ultimately failed. While her husband had a clean shot to his left temple, with no signs of having lived long enough to hit the floor.

That wasn't fair.

He deserved far worse than instant death.

My stomach rebelled, and I gasped a breath, turning

around and bending over to breathe slowly, steadily, through my mouth. In. Out. In. Out. As I focused on my breathing, Ben called the station, informing the Captain that they were both D.O.A. It was not the news either one of us had hoped to share, but that was part of the job. Having to share the worst possible news...

At the worst possible time.

I glanced over my shoulder again, breathing heavily, my eyes locked on the couple inside the home. This case hit way too close to home—especially considering what we'd been talking about on the ride here. All I could think, besides the fact that this never, *ever* should have happened, was...

That could have been me.

SIX

Ben

——————

$\mathcal{I}$ had no idea what the fuck I was doing right now. Sarah, in no way shape or form, ever gave me so much as a clue that she wasn't okay, or that she wanted me to show up on her door to check on her. Yet here I was, at her door, with every intention of checking on her. There had been something in her eyes as we said our goodbyes this evening that had stuck with me.

Something haunting.

Seeing Liz like that had been scarring, but I was kind of used to the horrible things people did to one another by now. I'd seen too much shit. Arrested too many monsters.

In a way, I was numb to the horrors I witnessed every day—I had to be to move on with my day. If I let the horrors of the world affect me, I wouldn't be able to do my job calmly and efficiently. I never lost my cool, would never hesitate to take a shot if I had to, and never took a shot when I didn't. In any situation, I knew what to do, and when to do it.

I took pride in that.

But seeing that look in Sarah's eyes...it had set me

straight on my ass. There had been something there, something hidden in those deep brown depths, that I'd been unable to ignore.

So. Here I was.

Shifting the six pack I carried into my other hand, I knocked softly three times. It was early still, only eight at night, but most of the lights were off in the house. Was she sleeping already? Footsteps sounded, and I felt her presence on the other side of the door.

Yes, that's right. *Felt.*

After such a long pause that I was sure she was going to pretend she hadn't heard me knock, the door unlocked with a *click*, and she opened it. "Rollins? What are you doing here? Is something wrong?"

Guess it had been too much to hope that her slip up with my first name would be permanent. "No, nothing's wrong. I just..."

When I didn't continue, she cocked her head adorably. She wore a pair of pajama pants with ducks on them, pink socks, and a strappy tank top that matched the yellow ducks. "You just what?"

Something told me if I admitted that I was worried that the case from earlier might have made her uneasy, due to her past with her ex, she would freeze up and push me out. I knew her as well as I knew myself, despite the years we'd been apart, so I didn't want to say that. Instead, I settled for a different version of the truth. "We started off on the wrong foot."

She crossed her arms and leaned on the door jamb, watching me from under her lowered lids. Jesus, her lashes were that long *without* makeup? "You mean, like when you said, and I quote, 'Hell no, I'm not being her partner. Pick someone else.' Is that what you're referring to?"

Wincing, I nodded. "Yes. That."

"Forgiven."

It was my turn to cock my head. "Just like that?"

"Just like that."

I snorted. "Yeah. Okay."

"This was fun, thanks for stopping by." She stepped back into the house and started to close the door in my face. "Buh-bye—"

"*Wait.*"

She blew out a breath and pushed her dark brown, almost black, hair off her shoulder. "What?"

"I brought you beer." I lifted my hand. "And takeout."

She frowned, staring at me. "Why...?"

The way she looked at my hand, as if she expected the food to jump out and pounce on her, made me stiffen. Had I been that much of a prick to her that she didn't even trust a *meal* coming from me? "Like I said, we started off on the wrong foot. I'd like to step forward on the right one this time. May I?"

She stared at me for so long I was starting to wonder if she'd been frozen in time. After what felt like a million years, she said, "Why are you doing this?"

"Do I have to have a reason?" I asked quietly, knowing damn well I did.

After all, I'd made it very clear I wanted nothing to do with her from the moment she'd stepped foot in my precinct.

She stepped back outside and crossed her arms. "Yeah. Start with why you're acting like I'm the one who messed up all those years ago."

"You left me without telling me—" I started, exasperation taking over any attempts I had at remaining calm and detached. I cut myself off, swallowing hard. Yes, she'd left me behind without an explanation, and yes, I'd loved her much more than she'd loved me, but that didn't change anything about here and now. She was my partner, for better or for worse, and it was time we both accepted it. End of story. "I mean, we both know what happened back then. That's not what matters, what matters is here and now."

"Yes, we do know what happened." She glanced behind her, nodded once, closed the door, then faced me. She squared her shoulders and pressed her mouth into a thin line, looking at me like she was ready to do battle. She wanted to fight? Fine, we'd fight. But I had *no* intention of losing. Not this time. "You cheated on me."

My jaw dropped, then I stepped closer. Out of all the things I expected her to say, it wasn't a blatant lie like that. "I did *what*?"

"You." She poked my chest, voluntarily touching me for the first time since she came back to town. "Cheated." A small push. I planted my feet so I didn't budge, which only seemed to annoy her more. "On." Another poke to the chest, harder this time. "*Me*."

Snarling under my breath, I caught her wrist. And I didn't let go. "The hell I did."

"Don't deny it." She tried to tug free, but I didn't budge. "I saw you."

"You saw *nothing*," I snarled, stepping closer, towering over her with my six-foot-three frame. She drew in a breath and held it as her nostrils flared slightly. "Because I never cheated on you. Why would I have? I had everything I wanted."

She tried to pull free again. It didn't work. "No one ever has everything they ever wanted."

"Yes, they do." I stepped even closer. So close, that I could smell her perfume. She still wore the same damn scent she'd worn when she had been mine. It was like a slap to the face, considering what she was accusing me of. "*I did.*"

She shook her head and stepped back, only to hit the front door, so it didn't do her much good. "Why are you denying it? It was years ago. It's not like we're ever getting together again."

"I'm denying it because I didn't fucking do it." I tried my best to keep my voice down. But it was hard. The fact that she *believed* her lies...

It was infuriating.

For the first time since she started accusing me of this horrible thing, she looked confused. Uncertain. "I saw you in bed with Tiffany Thorne."

I laughed. Straight up laughed. She was a fool. An utter, complete, beautiful, naïve fool. "*Tiffany?*"

"Yes. Tiffany."

Shaking my head, I closed the distance between us, not giving a damn about personal space. "You mean Tiffany, who's gay, and has literally no interest in men? That Tiffany?"

Her jaw fell open, closed, and opened again. "*What?*"

"Yeah. She's gay. She'd be more likely to be caught in bed with you."

"I would have known," she protested.

"No, you wouldn't have. No one knew but me. She trusted me with her secret, and we used to hang out a lot at parties because girls would leave me alone when she was with me, and I never had to worry about her falling for me, or getting the wrong idea. Because all I wanted was you." I flexed my jaw. "That night, you were working, and she needed a wingman, so I went. She met up with someone at the party we went to, got lucky, and I gave her my bed to use, because she really liked her."

"So, then, your bed..."

"Wasn't mine that night." I swallowed hard, locking eyes with her. "You walked away from me without a word for nothing, and *that's* why I blame you."

She said nothing.

Good. There was nothing to say.

SEVEN

Sarah

_____

*N*o. There was no way that hadn't been him in that bed. His hair. The way he'd been holding onto Tiffany. The way the sunlight had played with the darker pieces...

It had to be him. *Right?*

He let go of my wrist, resting both his hands on either side of my head, but didn't back off, or give me more breathing room. I was too distraught to really care. How could that not have been him? How could I have been so wrong?

"So. Let me get this straight. You saw me in bed with her, and you didn't think that maybe, just maybe, we should have talked it out?" His jaw flexed. "You don't think that maybe, just fucking maybe, after years of being together, you should have tried to figure out what the hell was going on? Before you, I don't know, just up and left for college all the way across the damn country without telling me why?"

"When you cheated on me?" I pressed my lips together. "No. I didn't."

"I didn't cheat on you," he said between clenched teeth.

I shook my head, stubbornly refusing to believe him. "I saw you. Your hair..."

"She has a thing for girls with short hair." He shrugged, staring down into my eyes. I couldn't look away from his. They were warm. Angry. Passionate. Addictive. "Bigger girls. Sporty ones. Maybe she had a similar build to me. Maybe she was tall. I don't know. But it wasn't *me*. I never would have done that to you. *Ever*."

I stared at him, breathing heavily, for the first time not so certain of what I'd seen in that bed. If he hadn't cheated on me, if he hadn't done the unforgivable...then he had every right to hate me as much as he did. I was the one in the wrong, not him. I'd been the one to ruin what we'd had, and broken his heart in the process, as well as my own.

That knowledge wasn't an easy pill to swallow.

Oh God, what did I do?

"I..."

What was I supposed to say? That I was sorry? That I'd made a huge mistake? That it was too late to fix it now, but if I could go back in time to change what I'd done, I would. But...would I? Aside from Vinnie, I'd been happy in North Carolina. I'd made lifelong friends, gotten an amazing degree, and had become the woman I was today while there. Would I change all that if I could? Would I go back in time and choose him instead?

When I remained silent, he shook his head, letting out a laugh. "So that's why you left me. Because I 'cheated' on you."

I nodded, still saying nothing.

I'd been so young. So hurt. I'd just...*ran*. Was that so bad? Did that make me a bad person, that my fight or flight instinct had kicked in, and I'd chosen flight?

At my continued silence, he locked eyes with me again,

staring down at me challengingly. If he was waiting for me to apologize, he'd be waiting a long time. I'd apologize *if* and *when* I deemed I should, and not a second before. After all, I'd done what I'd done because I thought he'd cheated on me. Now he was saying it wasn't true, but who said that was the truth?

Maybe he was still covering his ass.

He'd never liked being the bad guy.

Laughing again, he shook his head slightly as he backed off. "Guess it really doesn't matter anymore why we broke up, huh? It's not like we're going to pick up where we left off."

I snorted. I couldn't help it. Despite my attraction to him, and any lingering feelings that I would deny until I turned blue in the face if asked about, he'd been a complete and utter asshole to me from the second I stepped foot in the precinct. I'd sooner kiss a frog than him.

Or so I kept telling myself, anyway.

He stiffened, stopping his retreat. He hovered over me now, his arms half bent, his face level with mine so his breath fanned over my cheeks. His breath smelled like whisky and gum. There was something in the way he pressed against me, his shoulders to mine and his hands on either side of my head, that screamed of dominance. Despite my earlier thoughts about not wanting to kiss him anymore, something in my stomach twisted, and I held my breath because *oh my God*, I wanted to kiss him. Right here. Right now. Would he taste as good as I remembered?

No. Probably even better.

"What's *that* supposed to mean?" he asked slowly.

His voice was deep. So deep it literally sent shivers down my spine.

Craaaaap.

I should back down. Talk him out of whatever the heck was happening. Make sure that we didn't cross any lines, because there were about a million reasons why those lines shouldn't be crossed. But he was looking at me as if he'd been waiting years for this moment, and if I was a little honest with myself, so had I. It was time to clear the air.

Then, maybe, we could finally move on...

And be partners.

So, I opened my mouth, and spoke without caution... God help us both. "It means that you're right, and there's no way in hell I would want to pick up where we left off."

He laughed again, only it wasn't really a laugh. It was more of a...*challenge.* "Is that so?"

"Yeah. That's so." I rested my hands on his chest, laying them on his hard (*very hard*) pecs. Clearly, some things had changed about him. I'd be willing to bet he never skipped a day at the gym, whereas as a teen, he'd been more apt to never skip a day at his Xbox. "You're not exactly my type, Rollins."

He stiffened even more beneath my fingers. "I'm not..." he broke off, laughing again, and leaned in even closer. So close it would take little to no effort from me to close the distance between us and find out if he was still the best I'd ever had. "Your tastes have changed that much, huh?"

My heart thudded against my ribs, stealing the breath right out of my lungs, making my legs tremble with weakness. Or had he been the one to do that to me?

Moaning, my stomach tightened, and every nerve in my body demanded I rise on my tiptoes to taste his lips. Instead, I fisted my hands in his shirt, met his stare, and said: "No, you're the one who's changed that much. You're an asshole now."

"And you're a bitch now," he shot back, his tone hard.

I shrugged. "I'm okay with that."

"So am I." And just like that, whatever spell he'd been holding over both of us snapped, and he pushed off the wall with both hands. "But, hey. I'll see you tomorrow. Enjoy your dinner, it's your favorite...provided *that* hasn't changed, too."

I let out a breath as I watched him go, and sagged against my house, breathing heavily. As he left, all I could think was: *Damn it, I should have kissed him.*

EIGHT

Ben

I shouldn't have gone to Sarah's last night.

Ever since she told me she'd thought I cheated on her, I'd had a ball of rage roiled up in my chest, pushing me to confront her every chance I got so I could show her just how much of an asshole I really was. After all, she'd called me one, and she loved to be right.

I'd once loved to make her happy.

When we'd been together, I'd been the most loyal, loving, dedicated boyfriend in this whole fucking world. Anything she wanted? I gave her. Anything she needed? I found. I'd gone out of my way to take care of her, and to show her she never had to doubt me or my love. Never, not once, had I given her even a tiny reason to think that I might ruin that by cheating on her.

Not. Fucking. Once.

So to hear that she had "seen" me with another girl, and then packed her bags and left without telling me why she'd needed "space" to "think" for a week—something I'd given her despite my confusion, because, again, I gave her whatever the *hell* she wanted—was like a blow to the balls with those high-heeled shoes of hers she loved to wear despite how impractical they were in the office. To call me pissed off was the understatement of the century.

I was *livid*.

Typing quickly, I documented the details of Liz's gruesome murder, and the entire crime scene, pausing only when I sensed someone come up to my desk. Since I couldn't sleep, I'd come in early to get some work done. I'd been one of the only people in the office until now. Lifting my head, I frowned at my best friend. "What are you doing here so early?"

Hernandez scratched his head, looking at me weirdly. "It's not that early. It's eight."

"What?" I glanced at my phone, lighting up the screen. Sure enough, he was right. I'd been here for two hours already, and I hadn't even noticed the room slowly filling up with people. On their own accord, my eyes travelled to Sarah's desk. Her chair was empty. "I didn't notice."

"I could tell. You didn't hear me calling your name, asking if you wanted coffee." He set a cup on my desk, and slid it toward me. "So, I took that to be a yes."

"Hell, yes." I picked it up, kicked back in my chair, and grinned up at the man who'd been there for me for longer than I could remember. "Thanks, man."

"Anytime." He perched on the edge of my desk. "What's up?"

"Nothing, just catching up on some paperwork."

Hernandez flinched. "The murder case?"

"Yeah."

Hernandez readjusted himself on the desk, smoothing his khakis. He wore a plaid button up shirt and a tie, with his brownish-black hair spiked and looking a little wild.

"How'd your new partner handle her first violent case? We don't get many of those around here."

I set my pen down a little too hard, immediately cursing myself. I was showing too much. Giving too much away. It was no one's business how I felt about her—not even my best friend's. "Fine. She's pretty tough."

That, at least, was the truth.

"Good." He glanced toward the door, running his fingers through his hair. "Speak of the devil..."

I looked up with way too much enthusiasm for my liking. Today she wore a tight-fitting grey dress that hugged every curve of her body. One I'd tried so damn hard to forget. Her long brown hair fell over her shoulders in thick waves, and she'd painted her lips a dark red today. Her medium skin shone with what could only be magical powers, and she walked with a grace that put every other woman out there to shame.

I couldn't look away.

"Fuck me," I muttered.

Hernandez grunted in agreement. "She looks good. today"

I didn't agree. I didn't need to. "You got any hot cases?"

"Nah." Hernandez looked away from Sarah. Good. I'd been *this close* to punching the man who had been at my side my whole life because he'd practically been drooling over her. "We got a case yesterday, but it was a dud. Nothing on the books for now."

"How's Thomas doing?"

Hernandez winced. "Enthusiastically optimistic, as always."

Samuel Thomas was a young recruit who told anyone and everyone he met that he intended to change the world. His optimism was cute, if not annoying. He was fresh outta school, and ready to take on the world. In my opinion, he and Sarah would have made a much better pairing than splitting up me and Hernandez like the captain had.

Sarah came over, eyeing me cautiously. After our fight last night, guess it wasn't too weird she might be nervous around me. "Hey, Hernandez."

Hernandez nodded at her, shooting me a look out of the corner of his eye. "Good morning, Lopez. How are you doing?"

"Great," she said, flatly. She glanced at me again, the dark circles under her eyes even more prominent than yesterday. "Any calls this morning?"

"Not yet, I've just been typing up my report on Liz's case."

She nodded once. "I'll do the same, then."

"Okay." I hesitated, my grip on the coffee mug flexing. "Sarah?"

She stiffened, and turned around slowly. "Yes?"

"I meant what I said last night."

Biting her lip, she darted a quick look at Hernandez, then nodded jerkily. "Okay."

And with that, she walked away.

Again, I couldn't take my eyes off her.

It was becoming an annoying habit.

"What did you say last night?" Hernandez asked in a stage whisper.

"That I wanted to start over." I leaned back in my chair, sighing. "We're partners now, for better or worse, and I choose to try to make it better. To move past the...past."

Hernandez pursed his lips. "Not a bad choice."

"I also found out why she left. I'll fill you in when there's no ears around."

After glancing around the office, Hernandez stood. "Garyowen's, at nine?"

"Deal."

Once I was alone again, I glanced at Sarah. She sat at her desk, waiting for her computer to load. As she waited, she tapped her fingers on her thigh. She'd painted them maroon. For some reason, I couldn't look away from her fingers as they tapped. When I finally did, I locked eyes with her, and got caught dead-ass staring at my ex.

She blinked at me, confusion—or perhaps another emotion I couldn't name—coloring her cheeks. I lifted a brow at her cockily, trying to play it off, and turned back to my own computer.

I needed to pull my shit together.

NINE

Sarah

———————

*T*his whole thing was a horrible idea.

When I'd gotten home from a long, tension filled, awkward day at work that started with Ben making eyes at me, Grace had been there with Mom like usual.

What hadn't been usual, though, was Grace insisting I shower, change, and go on a blind date with this great guy that *"You would just love."* Though I tried to protest, and insist that I would rather stay home with my mom, like usual, Grace had said she could wait for the locks guy to come—I'd custom ordered locks to keep Mom from wondering off in the middle of the night—and had all but booted me out of my own house.

So. Here I was. Waiting for some dude I didn't know to show up...or not. Knowing my luck, the dude would stand me up. Then again, if he never showed, I could go home.

Ugh.

What if the locksmith had an issue installing the locks? What if my mother had another episode like she'd had in the middle of the night last night? Sleep had been hard to come by lately, and so had peace of mind, so the last thing I needed was to be here, waiting for some guy to show up so I could find out he was just as disappointingly selfish as all the other men I'd dated. But Grace had asked, and she was doing a lot for me, so I went.

My phone buzzed, and I glanced down. It was a call from an unknown number. Grimacing, I picked up. "Hello?"

"Hello, Sarah." The voice on the other end was crackly and broke up, so I could barely hear him.

I pressed my hand to my free ear, leaning down a bit to hear better. "Yes, is this Derek?"

"No." A short laugh. "Don't you recognize my voice, babe?"

I froze. My whole world, *everything,* froze. That laugh. That cold, careless tone... *No.* This couldn't be happening. Not now. Not after I'd finally gotten away from him. My heart unfroze, coming to life with painful acceleration. "How did you get this number?"

"Who the fuck is Derek?" Vinnie asked, anger seeping from every word.

I ignored his question. "You're not supposed to call me. You're breaking the Protection from Abuse Order I filed against you, and if you think I won't report it to Judge—"

"Go ahead. I'm not scared." He laughed again. "But *you* should be, and so should this Derek guy. You belong to me, and I don't share what's mine. You know that."

My stomach dropped. So many memories of him "punishing" me because some guy had checked me out came over me. Familiar, chilling and all unwelcome. "I'm *not* yours."

"I bet you look really pretty tonight. Are you wearing a dress?"

I shivered, glancing around the restaurant. Was he

here? Could he see me now? I ignored his questions again. He was just trying to get a rise out of me. It wouldn't work. He no longer held any power over me, and it was time for him to realize it. "How did you get out of jail?"

He laughed, not answering me.

After a period of silence, I broke it. "Don't call me again."

"See you soon."

I tightened my grip on the phone. "Then you'll go to jail."

"Maybe. Maybe not." He laughed again. That sound, that *horrible* sound, sent a shiver down my spine. "You shouldn't have gone home. It was too easy to find you. But, hey, for what it's worth? That color of purple looks amazing on you, babe."

Oh my God. He was here. He was actually *here*.

Hanging up, I stood, trembling. Spinning in a circle, I scanned the crowd, looking for him. Was he in this room? Watching? Planning? Plotting? Despite myself, and the strength I'd recently found after leaving him...I started to panic. Picturing his face on every man's face in this restaurant, sure he was about to come out and take me. "Oh God."

"Sarah?"

I swung around, my hand on my purse, which held my holstered pistol. I fully intended to aim it at Vinnie, if he was stupid enough to come at me in public, but it wasn't him. It was someone else who haunted me, but in an entirely different way. I grabbed his suit jacket, hanging on tightly. "He called me, Ben."

"Who called—?" Ben started to ask, but then he broke off and stepped closer. "You mean, *him*?"

I nodded frantically, swallowing hard "He found me. He's going to come for me, and this time, he won't stop until

I'm dead. He promised me one day he'd find me and kill me, and now he has. He's going to kill me."

Ben rested his hands on my shoulders. They were big. Warm. "I won't let that happen."

"You can't stop him. No one can." I held onto him tighter, panic taking over me. I couldn't breathe. Couldn't think. Couldn't process. Couldn't—just *couldn't*. "I'm going to die, just like Liz. He's going to find me, and kill me, and then you'll file the report."

"Never." Ben let out a growl, pulled me into his arms, and hugged me close. I knew it was bad to do this, to lean on him like this, but there was no way in hell I was letting go of him right now. I needed to know I wasn't alone. I...I needed *help*. "I won't let him. I swear to you, I will protect you from him, and I'll have your back."

I pulled back, staring into his dark green eyes. The way he watched me, with his arms around me tight, almost made me believe he could keep me safe. That he *wanted* to keep me safe, when I'd done nothing but be standoffish to him since we became partners. "Ben..."

He shifted closer, his grip on me changing ever so slightly. "Yeah?"

"I—"

"Sarah?" an unfamiliar male voice said from behind us.

I spun and stared at him, breathing heavily. There were so many emotions swirling inside me that I couldn't tell one apart from the other. Long lost feelings for Ben. Fear of Vinnie. Uncertainty about how to proceed from here on out. "D-Derek?"

Ben stepped in front of me protectively, his hand on his pistol. "Who the hell is this?"

"It's not him," I said quickly, resting a hand on his arm.

Ben immediately went at ease.

"Not who?" Derek hesitated. "Is something wrong?"

"N-Nothing." I stepped around Ben, trying to smile at the poor guy and failing horribly. "This is my partner, Detective Rollins."

They shook hands.

As Ben pulled back, I forced a smile. "I'm sorry, Derek, but can we get a raincheck? Something with...work...came up. That's why he's here."

Derek shifted his weight on his feet. "Of course. Sure. I'll call you?"

"Yeah. Thanks."

"Nice to meet you, man." Ben wrapped an arm around my shoulder, nodding once at Derek as he led me toward the door.

I should shrug free, pull loose of his hold...but I didn't *want* to. For just a second, I wanted to feel safe, like someone had my back. For just a second, I didn't want to feel so alone in this fight against Vinnie...and then after that second passed, I'd go back to being the strong, independent woman I'd become.

The one who didn't want *or* need a man to save me.

TEN

Ben

_____

Seeing Sarah like this—shaking, terrified, nervous—scared the fuck out of *me*. I wasn't too manly to admit when I was scared, and this was one of those times. Sarah was strong. She brought new meaning to the word independent, and she had never been hesitant to tell me to screw off when I deserved it. She'd come home, ignored all the doubt from the guys at the precinct, and even worked through the fact that her captain had paired her with her ex to try to scare her off.

She'd stayed. She'd fought. She'd won.

But now, with one phone call from a guy who would be better off behind bars then out on the streets, she was so terrified she couldn't stop shaking.

Yeah, that scared me. How bad *was* this guy?

If I was going to help keep her safe, if I was going to guard her back, then I needed to know exactly what I was dealing with. I led her toward my car, but she balked. "I drove here."

"We'll get your car tomorrow."

Her eyes widened. "Tomorrow?"

49

"You're spending the night with me at my house."

"No." She pulled free, shaking her head. "I can't."

"Not like *that*. I just—"

"*No*." She crossed her arms. She was steadier on her feet now. "I can't just not go home. I have to go back."

Clearly, I'd overstepped my boundaries. I hadn't been coming on to her, though. Just trying to help by making sure she wasn't alone tonight. "Okay, fine. Then you'll go home."

She hugged herself, staring at me with pinched lips.

"Could I maybe follow you home?" I hesitated. "Just to make sure you're safe. I know you can take care of yourself, but—"

She nodded jerkily. "I'd like that, actually. I'm not being a bitch, I just...I have to go home, is all."

I hadn't expected her quick agreement, or her words. Why was it so important she go home? "Okay, I'll walk you to your car, then follow you."

She headed toward her Ford, but pulled up short. "Wait, were you meeting someone here?"

"It doesn't matter."

"But if you had a date—"

"I didn't." I tried not to focus on the fact that *she* had. She wasn't mine, and hadn't been mine for years, yet I couldn't deny the hint of jealousy I felt that she'd been at Garyowen to meet another dude tonight. "It was just Hernandez. I'll let him know something came up."

"Don't tell him about this." She bit her lower lip, nibbling it like she always did when she was nervous. "I don't want everyone knowing about Vinnie."

Vinnie. That was his name. That was such a douche name. "I'll only tell people if you ask me to, but them knowing isn't a bad thing. The more people you have looking out for you, the better."

She shook her head. "No."

I didn't say anything. Just waited for her to unlock her car, then opened the driver's door for her after it beeped twice. I checked inside her car to make sure it was safe before moving aside. "I'll follow you. Give me a minute to get to my car, and lock your doors."

"I will." She slid inside, shooting me a look under her lashes. "Believe it or not, I know how to protect myself, Rollins."

My cheeks heated. "Yeah. I know." I walked toward my car, but only made it a few steps before I heard my name.

"Ben?"

I stiffened. "Yeah?"

"Thank you," she said, her voice quiet.

She shut the car door before I could reply, but there was really nothing to say. If she needed me, I was there. If she needed help, I'd be the first to offer it. Every time.

Guess some things never changed, huh?

As I pulled out of my spot, Sarah passed me, and we nodded at one another. I followed her home closely, watching for any hint of a tail on us. If that fucker even thought about harming so much as a hair on her head...he was a dead man. End of story.

Surely the douche was too smart to show up here, and go after a detective on her own turf. Then again, guys who beat on women weren't usually smart...or rational.

As I pulled into her driveway, I craned my neck and glanced at the house. Lights were on, and there was movement inside. I slammed the car into park and hopped out with my hand on my pistol, calling out to her, "Someone's inside your house. Stay there."

She fidgeted, closing her door. "I know."

"Oh." I approached more slowly, something she said making more sense now. "You have a roommate?"

"Something like that." She hesitated, nibbling on her lower lip. "My mother, actually."

I blinked. "You live with your *mother*?"

"More like she lives with me."

"Okay." At least she wasn't alone, then. Not that her mother was much bigger than her or anything, but I wasn't one to underestimate an angry Mama Bear. I glanced at her house again, only now noticing we weren't alone out here. Men worked on her front door, drills buzzing, voices low. "Are you getting new locks installed?"

"Yeah. Deadbolts."

I frowned. "On the top of your doors?"

"Yeah..."

When she said nothing else, I cleared my throat. Maybe that was my cue to get the hell out of here. Clearly, she didn't want me hanging around. "Well, if you're—"

"My mom has dementia." She fidgeted with her keys, not looking me in the eye. "It's pretty bad. I have a full-time nurse with her all day, Grace, and then I take care of her myself at night. The locks are to help keep her in at night, in case she tries to leave. They're password protected, so she can't slip out without me knowing."

I stood there, feeling like a complete and utter ass. I'd teased her about looking tired, about being out too late partying, and she'd been losing sleep over her ailing mother. *I'm such a fucking asshole.* "Shit, I'm—"

"Don't look at me like that," she said sharply.

I hesitated. "Like what?"

"Like you pity me. I don't need your pity. She's my mom, she needs my help, so I came." She flipped her hair over her shoulder. "You'd do the same for your mom."

I swallowed. "How does no one know about this?"

"Grace helped me keep it quiet."

Of course she did. "Why? People could help you."

"I don't need help," she said stubbornly.

"Everyone needs help," I argued, my tone low. "It's not a sign of weakness to ask for it, Sarah. It's a sign of strength."

She said nothing. Just swallowed.

"Is she why you came back to town?"

Nodding, she tucked her hair behind her ear. "She might not remember much, but she knows this home, and I don't want to take her from it."

Damn it. This only made old feelings for her stir up more. She was so noble, kind, and valiant, and she didn't even see it. Didn't even try. She just *was*. "She's lucky to have you."

She shrugged, averting her face. "I'm the lucky one."

I said nothing.

After a few moments of silence, she looked over her shoulder, then turned back to me. "Now that my secret's out, do you want to come in?"

"Do you *want* me to come in?"

"Grace is there. Would that be weird?" She bit her lip again. "I understand you guys had a thing once."

"I..." Shit. She knew about that? "It was a long time ago. One night. Meaningless on both sides."

She shrugged again. "Whatever."

For some reason, I felt like I should apologize, which was crazy, since she'd been long gone when we'd hooked up out of a night of loneliness and lust. We'd both known what it was—a scratch to an itch. Me and Grace had remained friends since, and neither of us wanted more than what we'd had. So, there was absolutely nothing to apologize for.

If I told myself that enough times, maybe I'd believe it.

She headed for the door. "You coming?"

Without replying, I fell into step behind her, following her just like I always had. She could invite me into hell, and if she was leading the way...

I'd be right there, trailing behind her.

Like the lovesick fool I was.

ELEVEN

Sarah

I handed the check to the locksmith, smiling at him. I could sense Ben hovering behind me, watching but saying nothing. He'd been stonily quiet ever since he came inside, and Grace left. Mom was sleeping, so that had made for a lot of awkward silence. "Thank you."

The man nodded and inclined his head. "Have a nice night, ma'am." He left, the last of his tools and the faint scent of his cologne trailing behind him.

The door clicked shut, and I took a deep breath, not turning around just yet. What had I been thinking, inviting him inside like this? What happened now that we were alone? What was I supposed to say? *Thank you for coming home with me? Please don't tell anyone about this? Why didn't you call me after I left?*

None of those seemed right, so I settled for the easiest thing I could think of. "Would you like a drink?"

He stood, swiping his hands on his thighs, hesitating. I could practically see the wheels turning in his head, calculating the pros and cons of accepting my offer. What did he think I was going to do? Jump him? He studied me, his gaze intense and his mouth pursed. After what felt like ages, he nodded. "Yeah, I'd love a drink."

"If you'd rather go—"

He frowned. "Sarah."

"Yeah?"

"I said I'd love a drink, and I meant it."

"Okay." Not saying anything else, I headed for the kitchen, my cheeks hot. There I went, overthinking everything again. "Beer or whiskey?"

"What kind of beer?" he asked from way too close behind me.

"Guinness." I glanced at him over my shoulder. "That still your favorite?"

"You remember my favorite beer?" he asked slowly, narrowing his eyes.

"Of course I do." I opened the fridge, taking one out and offering it to him. It felt cool against my fingers, a welcome change from the consuming heat inside me that threatened to eat me alive because his fingers were about to touch mine. "Back then we weren't old enough to drink it yet, but we won't talk about that."

"We weren't old enough for a lot of the things we did." He took the bottle from me, his fingers indeed brushing mine, just like I'd thought they might.

My stomach clenched into a tight fist, and I jerked back abruptly. "True."

He cocked his head at me. "Yeah."

After he cracked open the beer, he handed it to me, then reached past me into the fridge to grab another for himself. As he did so, his shoulder brushed against my stomach, and it took every ounce of self-control not to lurch back to ensure it didn't happen again. Every time he touched me, he awoke memories best left for dead.

"Speaking of things that we shouldn't have done, remember that night at the baseball field?" he asked out of nowhere.

I groaned and took a sip of the beer he'd given me. "How could I forget?"

"I can't believe you actually did it," he teased, grinning. When he smiled like that, his eyes lit up, and I instinctively moved closer to that brightness. To that warmth.

When we were still kids, he'd dared me to run the bases naked, and I'd done it. A few Guinness's had been involved in *that* decision, but when he'd laughed, stripped down, and joined in the fun, I'd never felt more alive. And when he'd backed me against the batting cage and pressed his open mouth to mine, I'd been sure my heart was going to burst into pieces. We'd been young, stupid, and in love. That had been a month before I'd "found" him in bed with another girl.

Staring at my beer bottle, I said, "I didn't want to back down from a challenge."

"Are you still that girl?"

"The one who runs bases naked?" I shook my head. "No. I follow the law now. It's kind of my job."

He leaned on the counter, crossing his ankles. He made such a simple position look so damn sexy. It just wasn't fair. "When's the last time you broke it?"

"Uh..." I bit my bottom lip, thinking hard. "In college, I tried pot once."

He choked on a laugh. "*Once?*"

"Yep, once." I tucked my hair behind my ear, refusing to be ashamed for being a law-abiding citizen. "You?"

"I tried it more than once in college." His lips twitched. "But never since I decided to become a cop."

"What made you want to be one?" I asked hesitantly.

When I'd told him I wanted to go to college for Criminal Justice, he'd rolled his eyes so hard I'd teased him about permanent damage. Last I remembered, he'd sworn to never become a stick-up-his-ass detective like his father, and yet here he was. With a stick up his ass like his dad. "Why did you change your mind?"

"I don't really know," he said with what struck me as complete honesty. "One day, I'm going to Somerton University for Business, and the next, I'm changing majors to Criminal Justice. I just thought about it, and realized that's what I wanted to be." He shrugged. "Guess I grew up, and stopped trying to be different from my father."

"Guess so."

He tapped his fingers on his bottle. "I thought you were going to go to law school?"

"When I applied to Duke, I still wanted to be a cop, so I got in under that major. I wanted to go, so..." I broke off, not looking at him.

"You wanted to go so badly, you were willing to change majors?" he finished for me.

I nodded, not saying anything. There was nothing to say.

"So." He stared off into the distance. "How long has your mom been sick?"

"It started getting really bad last year. I noticed little things, like she'd call me, confused about the day, or even the time. Then over the months, it got steadily worse. When I came home to visit last time, she asked me who I was. I immediately contacted a doctor, and they told me she was developing dementia, and that it would never go away. As of now, there is no cure."

He flexed his jaw. "Jesus."

"She doesn't even recognize me half the time. She

thinks I'm a nurse. The doctors said to roll with it, since it upsets her if I try to correct her, so when she asks me to check on myself—you see, in her head I'm still a child—I tell her I'm fine, and that I'm in bed sleeping with Mr. Annie, my favorite stuffed animal." I shrugged my shoulder. "It calms her down. I'll do anything to take care of her, to make her feel better, so I pretend not to be me."

He stepped closer. "But what about you?"

"What about me?" I asked, my heart picking up speed because he'd stepped even closer to me.

"Who is going to take care of you?" he asked softly.

I stiffened, alarm bells going off in my head. "Me."

"All by yourself, with no help." Another step closer.

"Y-Yes." I forced my feet to stand still. "I told you, I don't need help."

"Everyone needs help," he repeated. Another step had him directly in front of me. I had a little bit of room left to retreat, but I forced myself to stay still. "Were you going on a date tonight?"

"Yes," I said, confused at the sudden change in topic. "Grace set me up with him, I'd never met him before."

"Is now the best time for blind dates?"

I blinked. "Um... Why wouldn't it be?"

"Please tell me you're not on Tinder, or anything stupid like that."

Now I frowned. What the hell business was it of his if I was? "Why do you care whether I'm on Tinder?"

"I care because your ex could make a fake profile, or somehow fool someone who doesn't know him into setting up a date with you." He snapped his fingers. "Just like that, he'd have you."

Well, crap. I hadn't even thought of that. Grace had no clue what Vinnie looked like, so she easily could have made friends with him, and then set me up on a date. Far fetched? Sure. But I'd solved enough crimes to know it wasn't an impossible scenario. I could have easily walked into a trap tonight, and no one would have been able to save me.

Not even myself.

TWELVE

Ben

─────────

"**Y**ou're right, I shouldn't have done it. It's just..." She shifted on her feet, not backing off from me, but not exactly looking comfortable with our proximity, either. "I'm just lonely. Ever since coming back, people have been standoffish. I think most of them blame me for what happened between us, and they're letting me know it."

I clenched my teeth. I hadn't exactly made it any easier on her when she came back, either, so I got it. I understood her desire to meet someone. But *still*. Something inside me twisted at the idea of her seeing another man, but I tried my best to shove it down. "I'm sorry."

"Don't be." She shrugged. She stared at her beer bottle, picking at the label. "You stayed, I left. Naturally, they'd side with you." She paused. "And, if what you said is true—"

"It is," I said stiffly.

"—then I *am* the one to blame," she finished faintly.

Well, she wasn't wrong there. The anger I'd felt earlier today had faded, and I no longer wanted to scream at her, but when you emptied the bucket out and stared down at the dirty bottom, the truth was there to see. *She'd* jumped to assumptions instead of trusting me, and *she'd* run away without giving me a chance to explain, or defend myself. That had been shitty, sure.

But it had also been a long time ago.

It was time to move on, for both of our sakes.

"It's whatever. We were different people then."

She lifted her chin. "Yeah, we were kids."

"Babies, practically." I reached out and rested a hand on her shoulder. She was so frail, so tiny, and yet she held onto a quiet strength inside her that rivaled my own. She'd never been one to let life push her down, and I couldn't help but admire that about her. "I'd like to think now, as partners, we would give one another the benefit of the doubt, though."

She swallowed hard. Her brown eyes were dark and deep with worry and pain, and I had the insane urge to pull her into my arms and hold her close. To never let go. "We would. I would." She hesitated, then added. "I'm sorry for running away from you."

I swallowed hard. "I'm sorry for letting you."

She closed her eyes for a second, but not before I saw the sadness lurking in their depths. "Did I really give you a choice?"

"We always have a choice, Sarah." I cupped her cheek, my heart racing because her skin was as soft as I remembered. Would she still taste the same? Suddenly, it seemed incredibly important I find out. I lowered my head, unable to stop myself because she was looking up at me like nothing had ever changed between us, and like I'd never lost her all those years ago.

Christ, I wished I'd never lost her all those years ago.

She licked her lips and swayed closer. "Ben…"

Hearing her use my name snapped me out of it. I was pressing my luck, and the last thing either of us needed right now was to cross that line, and risk our jobs and partnership. She needed this job, and I needed to be her partner so I could keep her safe.

Dropping my hand, I stepped back and let out a long breath. "I'm sorry. I don't know what came over me."

She blinked, then seemed to come to her senses, too, because she covered her mouth and stepped even further away from me. "Yeah. Me too. Sorry."

"We can't..." I gestured between us. "You know."

"I know. I don't want to."

We stared at one another, breathing heavily. After a moment of silence, I downed my beer and stepped back even more. It wasn't enough, though. I could still feel that invisible electrical current urging us closer together. "Want me to sleep on the couch, in case he shows up?'

"You don't have to do that," she said immediately, her cheeks flushed.

"I know I don't have to." I crossed my arms. "I want to."

Opening her mouth, she started to speak, but cut herself off. She did this a few times before settling on, "Why?"

"Because I care about you."

Her jaw worked. "You...care...about me?"

"Of course I do." I cocked my head. "I mean, you're my partner."

She nodded, her grip tight on her mostly full beer. "R-Right."

"And I refuse to let some asshole come here and hurt you. Not on my watch."

She said nothing, just stared at me, face pale.

"Unless you don't want me here."

"It's not that." She cleared her throat. "What if people talk?"

"No one will talk. No one will know."

"In Somerton?" She rolled her eyes. "Everyone always knows."

"Fair enough," I admitted. "I'll tell the chief what's up, then." When she opened her mouth to argue, I held a hand up, silencing her. "I will swear him to secrecy. It's the best way to ensure that no one gets the wrong idea at the office. Besides, he's going to need to know about this. As your supervisor, it's his job to know if someone is threatening one of his detectives."

She didn't look happy, but she eventually nodded. "Fine."

"Would you like me to spend the night, Sarah?"

She hugged herself, glancing at the back door. "You're sure you don't mind?"

"Never."

Shivering, she shuffled closer to the kitchen entrance. "Then, yes, please spend the night. Not much scares me, but the idea of him out there somewhere, watching me..."

"I'll stay."

She started for the kitchen door. "I'll get pillows and a blanket."

I watched her go, rolling my hands into fists as I made my way to the back door, double checking the locks. I peered outside, looking for anything that looked out of place in the shadows.

Nothing.

I couldn't shake the look of fear in her eyes when she'd told me about her ex, and that he might be back in town. What had that monster done to her? If I ever got a chance to get my hands on him, I'd show him exactly what happened when you picked on females. Then I'd show him exactly what I thought of a "man" who was okay with hurting women, and scaring them into submission. If I ever got the chance to meet this son of a bitch...

My face would be the last thing he'd ever see.

THIRTEEN

Sarah

---

*B*en looked so *peaceful* when he slept. I stood beside him, a cup of French vanilla coffee in my hand with two sugars and cream, and watched as he dreamt. That used to be one of my favorite things to do whenever we managed to lie to our parents well enough that we could sneak in a sleepover together—I'd always wake up before him so I could watch him at his calmest. When awake, he was like a hurricane tearing through the Atlantic. Asleep, he had a quiet calmness about him that pulled me in, and didn't let go. Of course, he did that to me awake, too, but whatever.

We wouldn't talk about that.

He'd taken his shirt off sometime through the night, and the blanket was low enough to show that he'd developed quite the six pack over the years. He was rock hard, toned, and had a sparse spattering of blonde chest hair over his pecs, that taped off into a thin line that led all the way down his abs and under the blanket to his—

He stirred, his eyes lifting slightly.

Heart pounding, I quickly held the coffee out, trying my

best to not appear as if I'd been staring at him like a starved woman. "Good morning! Coffee?" I asked, sounding a little *too* perky.

Blinking, he sat up and dragged his hands down his face. By the time he lowered them, he looked fully alert and awake. Just like that. It usually took me a cup and a half of coffee to do that. "Yeah, sure, thanks." He took it and set it down on the table. "What time is it?"

"Seven."

Nodding, he stood. His abs flexed, and despite my best resolve, my gaze dipped low. God, were there *eight* of them? "Mind if I use the bathroom?"

"Of course not." I gestured down the hall, forcing my eyes back to his face. "I put a toothbrush in there for you. I had a spare."

He grinned, rubbing his abs. "Thank you."

"Sure," I mumbled.

He walked away, and much to my chagrin, the back view was just as nice as the front. Muttering under my breath, I quickly folded the blankets he'd used the night before, piling them on the side table nicely and rearranging the pillows. It had been nice of him to spend the night with me, but in the light of the new day, I'd found myself feeling a little stronger. Since I couldn't sleep last night, I'd used the time spent in my bed wisely. I came up with a game plan. First step? Install a security system. Second? Change my phone number. Third? Contact the local magistrate to give him a heads up. Fourth? Contact the judge in North Carolina, too, to let him know Vinnie was breaking his PFA rules. Fifth? Watch my back incessantly.

Go to work. Come home. Lock the doors.

No more blind dates. No more going out.

Sure, I might get lonely, but until he was caught and the

situation was taken care of, it was how it had to be. Being lonely was better than being dead, right? After all, who would take care of Mom if he got his hands on me?

Ben came back out, still shirtless, stretching. "Thanks for that."

"Thank *you* for staying." I crossed my arms and watched as he shrugged into his dress shirt, not buttoning it. "I don't normally need reassurance, but last night..." I swallowed. Was he ever going to button his damn shirt? "...I needed it."

"Anytime." He grabbed his coffee and came over to me. "I can stay as long as you'd like. Your couch is surprisingly comfortable."

"That won't be necessary." I lifted my chin. "I'm good."

"You're good." He frowned. "That can only mean one thing. You have a plan?"

He knew me so well. "I have a plan."

"Good. But my offer still stands." He reached out and caught my chin, stepping closer. "And you and me are gonna get this town to straighten their shit out. What happened between us was years ago, and everyone needs to get the fuck over it. We did, long ago."

I swallowed. "Yeah. Totally."

"I should have said something earlier, but if I see anyone giving you the cold shoulder, I'll give them shit." He ran his thumb over the curve of my jaw. "I've got your back, partner."

It was on the tip of my tongue to tell him I had my own back, and didn't need his help, since it came way too late, but I'd realized last night that he was right. I had to stop trying to do everything alone. I was only one person. "And I've got yours."

Our eyes locked, and something invisible charged

between us, sparking to life. My tongue swept over my dry lips, and I shifted closer without even realizing it. His grip on me shifted, as he moved his head slightly, dipping down to my level, but then he froze with his mouth mere inches away from mine.

Frustration hit me hard.

If I rose on my tiptoes...

"Shit," he growled.

"Sorry," I muttered, stepping back, my cheeks red.

That's *twice* I almost kissed him, and twice that he'd come to his senses before me, and rejected me. I needed to pull myself together. Despite our past together, he was my *partner*.

And partners didn't kiss.

He didn't let go of me, so I wasn't able to retreat far. "If you weren't my partner, nothing—and I mean *nothing*—would stop me from kissing you, right here, right now. I'd back you up against that wall, pick you up, wrap your legs around my waist, and find out if you're still the best kisser I ever had." He did exactly that. Backed me against the wall next to the entrance of the hallway. Too bad he didn't follow through with the rest of that mental image he'd given me. "I'd kiss you, run my hands over every delicious curve of your body that teases me every damn day, and by the time I finished with you, you'd never want me to leave. I'd make sure of it."

My stomach clenched tight. My legs trembled. My heart raced. And, God, I couldn't help it. I wanted him to do all those things, and more. "Is that so?"

"Yes, that's so. Because, damn, Sarah. These dresses you wear..." He slid his hand over my ribs, down my hip, and trailed off on my upper thigh. "...they fucking kill me."

I shivered, gripping his open shirt.

"But the thing is, I figure my dad put us together for a reason, right?" He gritted his teeth and retreated, not backing off completely but not quite close enough to kiss anymore, either. "My thinking is that he's hoping we slip up, and then he would have grounds for removing you from the force. He was pissed that he had to take you on because he wanted to hire his buddy's son instead, so if he has a reason to get rid of you..."

I blinked. "He'd get rid of me if we kissed?"

"Maybe. Maybe not."

"That's taking it a bit far." I pursed my lips. "Wouldn't he just, I don't know, reassign me to a new partner?"

"I honestly don't know. He can be pretty petty when he wants to be." He shrugged, stepping back. "I don't know about you, but it's not a risk I'm willing to take."

I cocked my head. "Would he fire *you*?"

"His son?" he asked hollowly. "Doubtful. But the new girl no one wanted to hire...?"

I frowned. "Ouch."

"Yeah." He rubbed his jaw, still staring. "Ouch."

As we silently weighed one another, the doorbell rang. After another moment of silence, I said, "That'll be Grace."

"We should probably let her in," he said hollowly.

I finally broke eye contact with him, and as I walked toward the door, I couldn't help but feel that whatever was going on between us was far from over. There was this pull between us, this animalistic attraction, that had never died. I was starting to think it never would, and sooner or later, this animalistic nature was going to win its battle with my self-control. Once it did?

I was going to be the one to lose.

FOURTEEN

Ben

——————

I couldn't get her off my mind. It didn't help that she was my partner, and that no matter what we did we were stuck with one another, but that wasn't what I couldn't stop thinking about. It was those almost kisses that kept getting to me. I'd never thought in a million years that she would come back to town, and look up at me like I was the one thing she regretted losing most.

Sure, I dreamt about it years ago, when she'd first left.

But those dreams had turned into reality eventually, then I'd realized she was never coming back, and she would certainly never want to kiss me again even if she did. Yet here she was, back in my life, in my arms, and I couldn't take what I'd waited years to get—

My second chance with her.

I glanced over at her desk. She hunched over it, biting her lower lip, typing on her keyboard quickly. Her brown hair fell over her cheek, hiding her face from my view, but what I saw of her profile was as breathtaking as always. She was everything I ever wanted and more, and I couldn't have her. It was enough to almost make me wish she had never come back.

Almost.

Standing, I walked right past her, nodding her way once as I made my way to the Captain—Dad's—office. I knocked twice, then waited.

"Come in," my father called gruffly.

I turned the knob and went inside, closing the door behind me.

Dad glanced up, saw it was me, and grunted. "Son."

"Hey." I crossed the room and placed a file on his desk. "Here's Liz's file."

"Thanks." He took it and placed it on the left side of his desk. "I'm still pissed off that it went down like that. We should have gotten there sooner."

"We got there as soon as we could. Me and Detective Lopez went as soon as you gave the orders."

Dad grunted again. "How'd she handle herself out there?"

"Excellent, sir." I hesitated, slipping out of father/son mode and into detective/captain mode easily. We had this whole dynamic down to perfection at this point in our lives. "Speaking of Lopez..."

"She's your partner," he said immediately. "I'm not changing it back."

"That's not it, sir."

Captain frowned and gestured for the chair in front of his desk. "Then what?"

"Confidentially, I found out why she came back." I cleared my throat and sat. "She was fleeing an abusive ex, sir." I kept mum on her mother's condition, as requested.

Dad leaned back in his chair. "Seriously?"

"Yes, sir. Last night the ex-boyfriend called her, freaked

her out, and I took her home and spent the night on her couch." I held a hand up. "Nothing happened, but I felt safer watching over the place. Having my partner's back."

The Captain nodded. "Good call. How bad is this guy?"

"She didn't tell me much, but knowing her and the way she was acting when he called her?" I let out a breath. "Pretty damn bad, sir."

"I may not have wanted to hire her, but I certainly won't allow her to get hurt." He pulled out a pen. "No one hurts one of ours. What's his name?"

"I only got a first name out of her so far. Vinnie. He lived in North Carolina, and she has a PFA against him, so I'm assuming it's on the books somewhere."

"I'll see what I can find."

I stood. "Thank you, sir."

"We'll place people on her house. Keep an eye on her until we find this guy and remind him he's supposed to stay away."

I hesitated. "I don't think she'll agree to that, sir. She's kind of independent, and doesn't want everyone knowing her business."

"Then why tell me?" he asked briskly.

"So you wouldn't think anything was going on with us, seeing as I spent the night at her house, sir." I rubbed my jaw. "And because we trust your discretion."

"I can't allow her to be unprotected. If she refuses to let the precinct know, then you'll have to be the man on her house every night until we find this guy. Sleep in a car, inside on the couch, tell her or don't tell her, I don't really give a damn. She's your partner, you decide on the best course of action, as long as she's protected." When I opened my mouth to argue, he quickly added, "That's an order."

He knew I didn't disobey orders, damn it. It wasn't in my DNA. Swallowing my protests, I saluted him. "Yes, sir."

"And son?" Dad added as I made my way toward the door.

"Yes?" I asked, not moving.

"Keep your hands to yourself." He set his pen down and steepled his fingers, staring at me with shrewd eyes. "We have a no-fraternization rule for a reason. Break it, and you will face suspension and possible termination. Just because you're my son doesn't mean I will let you get away with breaking the rules. If anything, I need to be tougher on you to avoid accusations of nepotism."

"Why did you partner us up?" I asked, unable to help myself. "Why put her with me?"

"Because she broke your heart, and came back here like it was nothing, demanding a job." He hesitated, and I inexplicably knew this was my dad speaking now, not my boss. "She doesn't get to have you again, not after what she did. This was my way to ensure she didn't get you."

I rolled my hands into fists. I'd been a mess after she left, sure, but I'd also been a kid, and it had been a long time ago. "I'm fine, Dad. What happened between us was a huge misunderstanding, and we have talked it out. She wasn't in the wrong any more than I was. I'm over it, and everyone else—"

"Yeah, well, I'm not, Detective." He glowered at me. So, the boss was back. All right, then. "Keep your damn hands to yourself, or pay the price, Detective."

I saluted again, biting back my anger. "Yes, sir."

FIFTEEN

Sarah

———

*T*wo nights later, I parked at the local gas station by my place and got out of my car, my steps brisk and short, matching my rapidly beating heart. No matter how fast I walked, or how many times I circled around the block, I couldn't shake the feeling that someone was following me. And, of course, if someone was following me, then my brain automatically went to the only logical place.

It had to be Vinnie.

As I walked into the gas station, I surveyed my surroundings. No one else was inside besides the teenaged worker behind the counter wearing a yellow shirt and a green vest. I walked through the aisles, pretending to look at things while really watching the parking lot and entrance for any familiar vehicles I might have seen during my drive. I hadn't spotted a tail, and yet I couldn't shake my intuition that someone was following me. That same intuition had yet to fail me, so I wasn't going to ignore it this time.

Hesitating, I pulled my phone out and clicked on Ben's name in my contacts. My finger hovered over the phone icon on the screen. Even though I knew I couldn't do this alone, I still didn't like going to him for help, but he'd assured me he was my partner, and that he was here for anything I needed. The past two nights, I hadn't needed anything, so I hadn't called or texted. But now, in the dark at a small gas station...did I need him?

I scanned the parking lot again. Nothing. Sighing, I tucked my phone away and shook my head at myself. Vinnie was winning. My own shadow scared me now that I knew he was watching me. I'd taken all the standard police protocol procedures for ensuring no one followed me, and had no reason to believe someone *was*. I'd give it another minute to be safe, buy something, head out to my car, and then go directly home to ensure I was safely inside.

Last night I'd gotten a security system installed, and it was fully functioning, so I was finally getting some sleep again. Thank God for small favors.

Ben and I had come to an understanding, too. He'd told me that his father was investigating Vinnie discreetly, and it was easy enough to admit I was grateful for the help, and the only reason I had that help was because I'd finally talked to my partner. Given our history, that hadn't been an easy thing to do, but it had been the right call. Now, we were on good terms, and we'd promised to be honest with one another from here on out.

Despite everything, I was grateful for him.

Never thought I'd say *that* again.

After grabbing a bag of Sour Patch Kids, I paid and made my way to my car, scanning the perimeter for any signs of malice as I popped a red one in my mouth. Those were the best ones, so I always ate them first, followed by the green. Ben liked the yellow and orange ones, so he'd always taken those. Out of habit, I picked around those, leaving them untouched.

As I munched a green one, I glanced over my shoulder. Nothing moved. All was quiet in Somerton, California tonight. The ride home was uneventful, and I almost made it home without incident when my phone rang over the Bluetooth, jarring my already fried nerves. I jumped hard enough to lose a red Sour Patch Kid. Glaring down at the dark floor by my feet where the fallen little guy lay, I hit the answer button on my steering wheel. "Detective Lopez."

Static sounded, but no one spoke.

"Hello?" I checked my signal as I drove through the wooded area that led to my house, frowning when I noticed I still had three bars. "Can you hear me?"

A crackle, and what could have been a word.

The hair on the back of my neck rose, but I tried to stifle it. I'd changed my number. It wasn't searchable on the Internet. The only people that had it were the precinct personnel, Ben, Captain, and Grace. There's no way he could have gotten my information twice in one week. This wasn't a horror movie, it was real life. This couldn't be happening. Not again.

Pressing my lips into a thin line, I hung up.

Not today, Satan.

I stopped at the stop sign down the road from my house, never feeling so isolated as I was now, in the woods, with not even a hint of the moon in the sky. I glanced in the rearview mirror for any signs of headlights, then turned left. I missed summer, when the sky didn't darken until nine. Now, in the beginning of fall, I was lucky to still see the sun at seven.

As I pulled up my driveway, my phone rang again. Unknown number. Stiffening, I clicked the answer button on my steering wheel. "Detective Lopez," I said, my voice sharp.

This time, there was no mistaking the sound of the stereotypical heavy breathing on the other end. It wasn't static, or even bad signal. It was a man. Breathing. Into the phone.

When had my life become *this*? When had I become trapped in this nightmare?

"Stop calling me."

Nothing. Just breathing.

I hung up again, trembling, and got out of my car, my hand on my gun. Walking quickly, I came to my doorstep and froze. There, lying on the porch, was a single red rose.

No note. No wrapping. Just a rose.

I'd never seen anything more terrifying in my life.

Rushing past it, I stepped on it, unlocked the door, and rushed inside, ignoring the flower that Vinnie had always given me when he "messed up" and "let me make him mad like that."

As I closed the door behind me, I called out, "Grace?"

Grace came out immediately, smiling. "Hey, how was work?"

"Good," I said, trying to keep my voice steady.

I hadn't told Grace about Vinnie, or his reappearance in my life, but maybe it was time. When Vinnie had come into my life, ruining it and everything inside it, I had become closed off to the world. All our mutual colleagues had taken his side, and hadn't believed my accusations. They'd made my life a living hell as I tried to navigate out of the nightmare I'd been in.

Out of necessity, I'd stopped opening up to people, and had trusted no one. But maybe Ben was right. Maybe it was time to change. "Can we talk?"

Grace frowned, looking worried. "What's wrong?"

"Nothing. I just need to tell you something about why I

left California." I sat at the kitchen table and motioned for Grace to do the same.

"Okay, but I have to tell you something first." Grace hesitated. "I don't know how long it'll last, since it's evening, but your mother has her memory tonight. You might want to go in while you can, and see if she remembers you."

I stood, trembling, the world spinning around me. "Seriously?"

"Yeah. Whatever you need to say can wait. I'll be right here."

Legs shaking, I ran toward to Mom's room, hope bursting in my chest for the first time since I'd come home. Over the last two months, my mother hadn't recognized me. Not even once.

So, if tonight was the night...

Was this *actually* happening?

I rushed into the room, slowing my steps as I came inside, making sure not to startle her. Mom's eyes landed on me, and I hesitated, not sure how to proceed. Mom had clearly showered, and she wore her favorite sweater and the necklace Dad had given her for her fortieth birthday.

She was knitting, like usual, but she'd started a new project besides the baby hats she usually made for baby me. Her eyes dipped down, then up, then down again, taking in every detail about me. Her eyes watered, and she opened her arms, smiling. "*Sarah*, my baby."

Choking on a sob, I didn't hesitate to run to my Mom. I flung myself into her frail arms and held on tight. She smelled just like I remembered. Flowers and perfume. Between my scare on the way home, the stress of my move, and now Vinnie finding me I just couldn't hold back anymore. When her arms went around me, holding me tight, there was no holding back my big, solid, loud sobs as my shoulders heaved with each one.

There was no stopping them.

She held me tight the whole time, brushing my hair off my forehead, *shh*ing me like she used to do when I was a child and I'd come home crying because Maggie Matthews had been mean to me at recess again. Eventually, the sobs stopped, and I forced myself to pull it together and not waste a single second of this time I'd been granted. The doctors had told me there would be days where Mom was lucid, and to not get my hopes up when they occurred, but this was the first time she'd actually had one.

I wasn't going to waste it crying on her shoulder.

Swiping my hands over my cheeks, I settled in on the edge of her bed. Mom's words from the other night echoed in my head, and I couldn't help but feel like I'd let her down. "I'm sorry for crying all over you."

"Nothing to be sorry for." She cupped my cheeks, smiling at me with her own watery eyes. "Such a beautiful woman you've become. I don't know how long we have together like this, so tell me *everything*. I don't want to miss a thing."

So...I did. I told my mother *everything*. I told her about California, and how I'd moved back here to be with her— but not mentioning too much about Vinnie, besides that I'd had a boyfriend back there, who'd turned out to be a jerk. Then I told her about being partnered with Ben, and how we'd made up recently.

I also told her that I was taking care of her, and swore I'd never leave her side, to which Mom had objected. "Grace told me how it's been. You shouldn't have to give up your life to care for me, Sarah."

"I'm not." I shook my head. "I have help. I have Grace."

"You could put me in a home. Visit me there—"

I held up a hand, cutting her off immediately. "No way. Absolutely not. I have you, and I'm not giving you up. Ever."

"But if it gets worse, if I become a danger to myself..." She squeezed my hand, smiling sadly. "If I become a danger to *you*? Please don't hesitate to put me in a safe place. If it's for the best, then so be it. You can still come visit me."

"Mom..."

"Promise me you'll do it, if it comes to that." She squeezed my hand, her grip surprisingly strong. "I need your word."

I hesitated, but finally nodded, giving her what she seemed to want. "But I promise I won't let anything happen to you."

After a while, and more catching up, Mom had faded off and fell asleep, and I left the room emotionally exhausted. Grace, true to her word, still sat at the table, a book in her hands and her feet up on the chair opposite her. When she heard me approach, she lifted her head and smiled. "I take it she was still lucid?"

"Yeah." I got two beers out and crossed the kitchen, offering her one silently.

Grace took it, twisting the top off. "I'm glad you got to see her like that, but tomorrow..."

"She'll be back to asking me if I'm a nurse." I sat heavily. "I know."

Grace took a sip of beer. "I'm sorry, Sarah."

"I know."

After a few moments of silence, Grace cleared her throat. "So... You said you wanted to talk to me?"

"Yeah."

Grace set her beer down and swiped her hands on her scrubs. "What's up?"

I hesitated, rested my elbows on the table, and locked gazes with my former best friend. The girl I used to trust with all my secrets. Could I trust her now? Guess there was only one way to find out. "You need to know why I came back here, besides for my mom, and what I'm running away from. It's time I told you everything about what happened in North Carolina."

Grace settled back in her chair. "Okay. I'm listening."

SIXTEEN

Ben

——————

*"Y*ou're kidding me, right?" I asked, my grip on my iPhone tight.

Dad sighed. "When do I ever kid about this type of thing, son?"

I glared at Sarah's house, staring at the only light that was still on—the one in her living room. Grace had left an hour ago, and I was in my customary position outside the house where I could watch over her without her knowing. I'd decided to keep my distance as I watched over her, because if I told her the truth, she'd insist I leave, and I'd refuse. We'd fight about it after my refusal, of course, but I was stubborn as hell, and eventually she'd see I wasn't going anywhere. Once she accepted that, she'd invite me to sleep on the couch. But if I slept on the couch, I'd be close to her, and if I was close to her, then I'd want to talk to her. If I talked to her, I'd want to touch her. And if I touched her, I'd want to kiss her. If I kissed her...we all knew what came next.

Yeah. Neither of us could afford that mistake.

"She should have told us."

He sighed. "I think it's time you press her for more information. The more we have, the better equipped we'll be to protect her. Are you there now?"

"Yes, in my car."

"Knock and pretend you stopped by. Tell her what we know, and politely request for the full story this time. We need to know exactly what we're up against here, and the only way to know that is the truth. From what I can tell, they dropped the charges, and accused her of fabricating the whole story, which means she lied about him being in jail in the first place. I want to know why she lied."

I gritted his teeth. "Yeah. Okay."

"Find out, or *I* will."

I nodded once, recognizing that tone for what it was— an order from my boss. "Yes, sir."

We hung up, and I sighed, shoving the phone in my pocket. Without wasting time on a game plan, I got out of my car and made my way up to the door, scanning the perimeter as I went. Nothing moved, or made a sound out of the ordinary, but I felt like someone was out there, watching. I didn't like that feeling at all. As I climbed the steps, I frowned at the trampled red rose on the porch. Had Sarah dropped it on her way inside?

Bending down, I picked it up, walked to the door, and knocked three times, sharply. Silence greeted me, then after a while I heard the lock unlatch, and she peered at me through the crack of the door. She wore a pair of duck pajamas, her hair was loose around her shoulders, and slightly damp as if she'd showered recently. Heart pounding because she looked so fucking adorable in those stupid pajamas, I held the rose out. "Hey. I—"

"What are you doing?" she said at the same time.

As her gaze fell to my hands, her eyes narrowed. She

reached through the door, snatched the rose out of my grip, and tossed it into the bushes.

"What the hell—?" I started.

"Why were you holding that?" she snapped, interrupting me.

"I found it on your porch, and picked it up." I looked over my shoulder at the bush that now hid the rose, confused. "Why did you throw it?"

"Because I don't want it." She stepped aside, and gestured for me to come in, searching the shadows much like I just had. Did she sense a presence, too? "What are you doing here?"

"What's with the flower?" I asked again as I passed her, watching as she shut the door and immediately locked it, then punched in the code for her security system. It beeped twice.

"I don't like roses."

I blinked. "Since when?"

"Since Vinnie used to give them to me after hitting me," she answered without hesitation.

"Shit." I stiffened, looking at the door. "Is it from him?"

"I don't know. I'm trying to tell myself it isn't." She hugged herself. "Why else would a random rose be on my porch, though?"

"You should have called me," I said, my tone hard.

"I was busy."

Busy. *Riiiight.*

Walking inside, I headed toward the couch where I'd slept the other night. Guess it would be my bed again tonight. No way in hell I'd be leaving her alone after hearing her ex may or may not have put a rose on her porch. "Is your mom asleep?"

"Yes, has been for hours." She hugged herself harder. "Why?"

"Because we need to talk."

"Says who?" she asked, trailing behind me.

"Me." I hesitated. "And the Captain."

She crossed her arms, eyeing me cautiously. "Why?"

"You didn't tell us the whole story, Sarah."

"I told you everything you needed to know," she said slowly, edging closer to the wall. She leaned against it, her arms still crossed, but I couldn't shake the feeling that she was seconds from fleeing me and my questions. "I dated him. He seemed like a nice guy. After a while, he started hitting me. Threatened my life and my job if I told anyone. Almost killed me. I finally left him, got a PFA, and then I came home."

I approached her cautiously. "But you left out one tiny little detail about him that was kind of important."

She lifted her chin, her eyes flashing defiantly. "What's that?"

"That he's a fucking cop." I stopped just short of touching her. "And that you turned him in, which made the department eager to be rid of you, which helped you get the job here. Oh, and you also lied, because he's not in jail like you said."

"There was no lie." She pushed off the wall. "Clearly he got out."

"No." I backed her against it by moving closer. She wasn't going anywhere until I had some answers. "He never got *in*."

Her nostrils flared. "What?"

"He was never in jail," I said rigidly. "You lied."

She pushed off the wall, ducked under my arm, and

started pacing furiously. "I didn't *lie*. Don't you dare accuse me of lying."

The way she said that, her tone broken, reminded me of something my father had said. No one had believed her, and she'd been all alone after she told the truth about her partner. Clearly, in my anger, I'd struck a chord—something I didn't intend to do. "Sarah...he was never in jail."

"You've got to be kidding me?" she cried, her face flushed with anger. "You're telling me the *second* I left, they just let him off the *hook*? They just let him *go*? They assured me if I left, if I went across the country—"

"So you actually thought he was in jail?" I interrupted.

"Of *course* I did." She stooped pacing and spun on me. "Why would I lie about that?"

"I don't know. Why would you lie about him being a cop?"

She poked me in the chest. "I didn't lie. I just didn't mention it. His profession is irrelevant to the situation."

"The hell it is." I caught her arm. "He was your partner."

"So? We didn't have a no-fraternization rule like your father." She tried to yank free, but I didn't let go. "I did nothing wrong, Ben."

"I never said you did."

"And yet you're looking at me like that," she spat, trying to pull free again. "With judgey eyes. Or is it that you don't believe me anymore? Are you like them? Are you going to accuse me of making it all up for attention?"

Anger hit me in the chest for more reasons than one. I backed her against the wall, releasing her, but not setting her free. Instead, I pinned her in with my body—which was probably a huge fucking mistake. "Are you seriously asking me that?"

"Are you seriously *looking* at me like that?"

I growled under my breath. "Like what?"

"Like I did something *wrong*." She slammed her hands against my chest, leaving them there. "They all looked at me like that when I reported him to the bureau. What was I supposed to do? Keep quiet? Let him kill me, because, hey, at least I wasn't turning in my partner, right? At least I wasn't turning on a fellow cop like a traitor?" She tossed her hair over her shoulder, staring up at me with fire in her eyes. "That's why you're looking at me like that, right?"

Shaking my head, I bit my tongue, trying to keep the words from coming out. If I told her why I was looking at her *like that*, there would be no going back.

"Then why?" she persisted, clearly not aware of how close I was to saying the worst thing I could possibly say right now, considering her body pressed against mine in all the right places, and all I wanted was to pull her into my arms, kiss her, and swear I'd never let any asshole hurt her again.

"I'm not looking at you like anything," I gritted out.

She shook me slightly, her grip on my shirt tight. "Yes, you are. *Why?* Tell me!"

Something inside me snapped, giving way to the need to be one hundred percent honest with her, no matter the consequences. "Because you should have been with *me*, damn it. Not *him*. You should have been *mine*, you should *still* be mine, and *I* never would have hurt you like that. That's why I'm looking at you like that—because I want you to be with *me*. I want to keep you safe, and I wish like *hell* we could go back in time, and do it all over again so you never left me."

The second I finished that sentence, I knew I'd made a huge mistake. But there was no taking them back now. I'd said them. I'd meant them. There was nothing to do about it.

Before I could even attempt to clean up the shitstorm I'd just unleashed on us both, she did the unthinkable. She rose on her tiptoes, closed the distance between us, and kissed me.

And I, selfish dumbass that I was, matched her unthinkable action with one of my own. Instead of pushing her away and ending it before things went too far, I closed my arms around her, hauled her against my chest, slammed her against the wall, and...

I kissed her back.

SEVENTEEN

Sarah

———————

*H*e backed me against the wall, his unyielding mouth claiming mine in a way no other man had ever managed to claim me since I'd walked away from him all those years ago. His hard body pressed against mine pushed me over the edge of control and logic. There was no longer any thought process, or hesitation. I'd wanted him from the moment I laid eyes on him again, and there was no changing that—especially not when his mouth was on mine.

His hands roamed down my curves, over my hips, and cupped my butt as he lifted me and backed me firmly against the wall. I moaned into his mouth, grabbing his shirt and yanking it up. I desperately needed to feel his skin under my fingers, to relearn what it felt like to have him. He obligingly broke the kiss off long enough for me to remove the shirt, and took advantage of the opportunity to haul mine over my head, too, without hesitation.

No complaints about that on my end.

He froze as he dropped the shirt, and for a second I thought he'd come to his senses, but then he slowly trailed his fingers up my ribcage, leaving goosebumps in his wake. "You're so fucking beautiful, Sarah."

I swallowed hard, not sure what to say, but luckily, I didn't have to think of anything. He melded his mouth to mine again, and I ran my trembling hands over his hard biceps. Every inch of his body had been chiseled to perfection, and it was hard not to be a little self-conscious about the fact that I hadn't been wearing a bra under my shirt, and that I was now topless in front of a man who by all accounts and purposes hadn't skipped a day at the gym for years.

Why'd I eat *all* that chicken at dinner?

But all those lingering thoughts went away as he closed his palms over my breasts, running the sides of his thumbs across my hard nipples. I dug my nails into his skin, opening my mouth to his. As soon as my lips parted, he slid his tongue inside, tasting me without any signs of the doubt that had plagued me. And just like that?

I doubted no more.

Instead, I relearned his body as his tongue and fingers drove me to heights I hadn't seen before. Everywhere I touched was rock hard and incredibly addictive, and I couldn't get enough of the way his crisp chest hair felt under my fingertips. I eagerly followed the trail of hair down his chest, over his abs, and to his waist. When I hit his belt, I hesitated, not sure whether to undo it, or wait to see if he came to his senses...

As if he heard my thoughts, he ended the kiss, dropped me down on my own feet again, and stepped back once I was steady. He kicked his black shoes to the side and undid his belt without taking his eyes off me, pausing only to remove a condom from his pocket before letting his pants hit the floor. Clothed only in a pair of boxers, he flexed his jaw, his hands fisted at his sides. "I'll only ask this one time, Sarah. Are you sure you want to do this?"

I swallowed hard, taking in every detail about him. His broad shoulders. The hard pecs with a coating of blond chest hair. His narrow waist, and the happy trail that begged me to keep following it, no matter what might happen if I did. But more than all that, I couldn't look away from the look in *his* eyes. He looked at me as if he might die if I changed my mind and walked, but he'd still pulled back long enough to give me the opportunity to do so.

Because that's the kind of guy he was.

Smiling, I tugged my pajama pants down until I, too, stood in nothing but my underwear. "I've never been more sure of anything in my life, Ben."

He swallowed hard, his jaw flexing. Before I could so much as blink, he was on me. His mouth collided with mine, shooting off sparks, and he trapped me between the cool wall and his hard, hot flesh. The contrast was downright tantalizing. He cupped my breasts, squeezing them with the perfect amount of pressure as he moved his hips against me, brushing against me in all the right places. I scratched my nails down his back, skimming over his shoulders and spine, not stopping until I reached the top of his boxer briefs.

Once there, I hesitated only a fraction of a second this time before sliding over his hips, to his stomach, down the happy trail, and inside his boxers. I closed my fist over his cock, squeezing the head and tugging gently. He groaned and thrust into my hand, his own slipping lower down my body to reciprocate my soft touches. When he teased my flesh, circling over where I needed him most without touching me with enough pressure to relieve my need, I moaned into his mouth, tugging on him harder.

"*Ben*..." I whimpered into his mouth, needing him to give me more, like, yesterday.

That seemed to be all the encouragement he needed. Breaking off the kiss, he dropped to his knees, putting him face level with my belly. He yanked my underwear down my legs, lifted my right knee, tossed it over his shoulder, and buried his face in between my thighs, sending me straight to heaven without a warning.

His tongue moved over me with a perfect rhythm that sent me soaring higher with each stroke, while his hands skimmed over my bare skin everywhere he could reach. My thighs. Waist. Breasts. My butt. Nothing was safe from his torment.

Every stroke, every graze, set my nerves on fire even more. Every muscle in my body tensed and strove for release, begging for him to give me what only he could. I strained to get closer to him, pumping my hips slowly as I grasped for the unreachable until it was suddenly there, in my grasp, and lights burst into my vision as I came hard.

I pressed against his mouth, riding out the wave, and then sagged against the wall, breathing heavily. As I tried to see straight again, he rolled a condom onto his engorged cock, taking care of the protection aspect of what we were about to do. I swallowed hard, my heart pounding a loud staccato against my ribs. It wouldn't slow down. Wouldn't calm.

Sure, I'd been with him before, but we'd been little more than children. Clearly, he'd learned some tricks over the years since I'd been gone. I tried not to let that bother me, because I'd learned a few tricks of my own, but jealousy crept up anyway. It was my fault he'd learned this stuff without me, and that was something I'd never forgive myself for.

He picked me up, backed me against the wall, kissing me just as frantically as he'd done before he sent me shooting into the sky. Then he drove inside of me, filling me completely, and I clung to him tightly, with no intention of ever letting go again...

Even though we both knew full well I'd *have* to.

EIGHTEEN

Ben

———

*H*aving Sarah in my arms again was like realizing I'd been asleep for the past ten years, and what I thought had been reality was in fact a dream. But now I was awake and I remembered what it felt like to be truly alive again. To breathe and laugh and *feel*. Now that I'd found that feeling again, now that I'd woken up, I didn't want to fall back asleep. There were a million reasons why we shouldn't be doing this, and a million and one reasons why it would never work...but there was also one huge reason why I didn't give a damn.

It was Sarah. It was *always* Sarah.

I thrust inside her, holding onto her tightly as I kissed her with every ounce of need I'd been feeling since the moment she walked back into my life, hating me because she thought I could have cheated on her. Her body closed around me, squeezing me, and I moved inside her at a steady rhythm, letting instinct take over. Every muscle inside me tensed, demanding release, but I refused to get there until I brought her to orgasm at least *one* more time.

As I moved inside her, I slipped my hand between us,

rolling my fingers over her. Memories of her fucking my mouth with wild abandon hit me, doing nothing to calm my demanding body down, but there was no shutting those images down even if I wanted to—which I, of course, *didn't.* I'd be replaying that memory in my mind for the rest of my life.

I deepened the kiss as I thrust inside her again, groaning when she writhed against me, her walls clenching down on me even tighter than before. She tasted as good as I remembered. Like happiness and heaven, all mixed into one. That didn't make any sense, but I didn't give a damn.

As my fingers moved over her wet skin, she cried my name into my mouth, digging her nails into my back so hard it hurt, just the way I liked it. Her body closed around mine, squeezing me in all the right places, bringing me dangerously close as she tumbled head over heels down the edge of pleasure. Growling, I finally let myself go, fucking her without a hint of self-control or calmness. I thrust inside her sweet body—faster, *harder*—and she cried out again, her body tensing around mine as she strained to reach orgasm one more time. When she got too loud, I silenced her cries with my mouth, holding my own pleasure back until she came again.

Pressing my fingers against her already sensitive core, I thrust inside her once, twice—*bam*, she came. This time, I was right there with her, blackness washing over me as I came so hard I forgot who I was and where I was for a brief second, but never who I was with.

Sarah. *My* Sarah.

Resting my forehead on hers, I kissed her sweetly one more time before pulling back to survey her face. I'd gotten a little rough at the end there, and couldn't help but wonder if I'd been a little *too* rough. I searched her face for any signs of pain or regret, but her dark brown eyes were glowing with happiness, and her skin flushed with pleasure.

Pleasure I'd put there.

"Wow," she breathed, smiling shyly at me, which was a little absurd considering I was still buried inside her body, but whatever. "That was amazing."

"Agreed," I managed to say, my voice still raspy. I touched her cheek, pushing her dampened hair off her sweaty skin. That simple movement, and the way she leaned into my touch with her eyes shut, hit my chest like a fist. It somehow felt even more intimate than what we'd just done. "I know this is a mess of complications we didn't need, but I don't regret a damn second of it. I refuse to pretend otherwise."

"Me, too." Her lids drifted up. "I don't regret it either."

I hesitated to ruin the mood, but shit had to be said. "But we—"

"I know. No one can know."

I swallowed hard. "I can't lose you as a partner. Not now."

"I don't want to lose you, either," she practically whispered, not meeting my eyes.

To be honest, I wasn't sure what to say. We couldn't be together, but we didn't want to be apart. There was no happy ending to this. No easy out. No obvious answers. What the hell were we supposed to do? "I need to be with you to watch your back. I don't trust anyone else."

"I know. This... It won't happen ever again." She licked her lips. "It can be a one-time thing, a goodbye of sorts."

Hesitating, I opened my mouth, closed it, and opened it again, shifting my weight slightly as I debated my response very carefully. I didn't want this to be a one-time thing, not at all, but aside from sneaking around behind everyone's back at the precinct, including my father's, was there really another option? "Is that what you want this to be? A good-bye?" I asked, my throat thick.

She bit her lip. "Don't ask me that."

"Why not?"

"Because you won't like the answer," she said, holding onto my biceps. "I care about you, Ben. I do. But I've been down this road before, and your dad kind of has it right. Dating your partner is never a good idea. It...complicates things."

I swallowed back my protests about not liking her answer, and focused on the one I should voice out loud. "I'm not him. Don't fucking compare me to him."

"I'm not," she assured me quickly. "I never would."

I said nothing, because it sure as hell sounded like she just had.

"But despite how much we like one another, despite our past feelings, we can't risk everything, right?" She studied me closely. Too closely. "We can't lose our jobs because we used to have feelings for one another, once upon a time."

What else was I supposed to say to that? That I still had feelings for her? That I'd give up anything for her, if she gave me the slightest clue that she wanted me to? It didn't matter if that was true, because for us to work, she needed to want *me* as badly as I wanted *her*, and that just wasn't going to happen. If it was, she wouldn't be pushing me away right now. "Right."

For a second, she looked upset. As if maybe she wanted me to go ahead and lay it all on the line, but she closed her eyes, took a deep breath, and anything I may or may not have seen was gone when she looked at me again. For all I knew, it had been a figment of my imagination. More than likely, it was. "So, then, this is goodbye."

"Well, not completely. We're still par—"

"But it is." She framed my cheeks with her hands, locking gazes with me, and my heart twisted in my chest painfully. "This is the moment when we move from what we were, what we could have been all those years ago if things had been different, and now we have to become... partners who have one another's backs, no matter what."

If that was what she wanted, if that was what she needed from me, then I'd give it to her. I'd sworn to myself, and to her, on that football field in junior year, that anything she needed, I'd give to her. She'd needed space to think, and go to college across the country? I'd given it to her. She'd needed a partner when she came back, running from a crazy ex, and caring for her mother? I'd given her that, too. Closure? Sure, I'd take my clothes off and give her that.

Now...she was asking me to give her a *partner*, and nothing else, so guess what? I'd make sure she got what she needed. It's what I did. Took care of her.

Swallowing hard, I stepped back from her, pulling out of her body for the last time. Guess it was my turn to walk away now. To deny myself of the only thing I'd ever wanted in my life—*her*. Holding my hand out, I forced a calm smile I didn't feel as we stood in her living room, naked and covered in one another's sweat. "To being platonic partners?"

She eyed my hand, then slid hers into it. "To being partners."

God help us both.

NINETEEN

Sarah

_____

The next afternoon, we sat in Captain's office, staring at him as he read my file, trying not to stare at one another as he did so. Last night with Ben had been...yeah, it had been incredible. The things dreams were made of. I'd never felt the way he made me feel—alive, vibrant, *wanted*—with any other man, and I had begun to suspect I imagined the whole thing. That all those memories of coming to life in his arms had been the childish fantasies of a girl who'd loved a boy with all her heart, and that the reality of the subject had been far duller than remembered.

One night in his arms had robbed me of that notion.

Being with Ben was like chasing a violent storm. I knew it might hurt me, and there was a chance I'd end up sucked into an endless void, but I did it anyway because guess what?

The risks were worth the reward.

If he'd wanted more than a one-time thing, if he'd wanted to keep on seeing each other in secret, I had a feeling I would have done it, despite the consequences. I would have given it all up for him, but in all honesty, I was happy he hadn't asked me to do so. To risk everything was to put my ability to care for my mother in jeopardy, and I couldn't do that. I could risk it all for myself, but not my ailing mother. It was better this way...

Or so I kept telling myself.

But having him at my side, dressed in his usual suit and button up shirt, was killing that thought process in my head, because he looked good enough to lick. He'd slicked his blond hair slicked back and slightly to the side, the way I liked it, and those arms that had held me up as he brought me to pleasure repeatedly were bulging against his suit jacket, begging to be set free.

I couldn't stop staring.

One taste of what things had been like with Ben wasn't enough. It would never be enough. And yet...it *had* to be enough. I couldn't risk losing my job, and having to move my mother out of her home. I couldn't just get a job in another town, since it was imperative I remain close to my mother in case of emergencies. There was no way this worked out happily for us, yet I knew instinctively that if we did this, if we ignored caution and gave us a try, we'd be happy. Truly happy.

Life wasn't *fair*.

I glanced at Ben again, unable to help myself.

He'd been staring at me, but when I looked at him, he jerked himself slightly as if he realized he'd been staring, sat up straighter, and winked cockily at me.

I forced a calm smile in return.

Captain lifted his chin. "Did no one stand by your side after this went down?"

"No, sir." I gripped my knees. "No one."

"And your partner?" he asked, staring at me as if he hadn't watched me grow up, and as if I hadn't sat at his table every Sunday night for dinner. "He went to jail?"

"I was told he would, sir," I said slowly, glancing at Ben. "But then Detective Rollins informed me that never happened, and he was free to stalk me as he chose."

Ben flexed his jaw. "A freedom he is clearly taking advantage of, sir. There was a rose on her porch yesterday, something he used to give her after...after...beating her. And there's been phone calls, too."

I side-eyed him. I'd told him that in confidence last night before he'd left, but Captain had requested full details, so I guess it was time to give them. "I don't have any proof either of those things were him, though, besides my instinct."

"They were him," Ben said without a hint of doubt.

His certainty matched my own feelings on the matter.

"I've got some more bad news," Captain said slowly.

I hesitated, glancing at Ben for any hints of what might be coming. He looked as interested in this information as me, so I guess this was news to him, too. Had he found out about what happened last night already? Was I about to get fired? There was only one way to find out. "And what might that be, sir?"

"He got the PFA thrown out on grounds of slander and libel." He hesitated. "After you left, he proceeded to plead his case with the judge, who, from what I hear, is in his pocket."

I stiffened, my heart tearing. "He is. But I never thought..." I broke off, taking a second to gather myself. "So, what you're saying is there's nothing stopping him, legally, from showing up on my doorstep."

Ben stood up. "Son of a bitch—"

"Sit *down*, Detective," Captain ordered.

Ben sat immediately.

I didn't move, too numb to even try.

"You are correct, Detective Lopez. There's nothing stopping him."

No wonder Vinnie had sounded so cocky on the phone when I threatened to call the judge. Heck, I had called him. No surprise that Judge Roberts had failed to inform me of the fact he'd let his drinking buddy off the hook without so much as a speck on his record.

"He can get me," I said hollowly.

Captain nodded, his eyes showing sympathy for the first time. "But I'll do my best to make sure that doesn't happen. Would you think it wise to consider a transfer to another state? Somewhere that he won't be able to find you?"

I shook my head. "No."

"But—"

"She's in the system as a detective. No matter where she goes, he can find her," Ben argued, his fists clenched tight. "With all due respect, that's not a solution...sir."

He hesitated. "New career?"

I said nothing. Just stared.

Ben cursed under his breath.

"If you insist on staying where he knows how to find you—"

I gripped my knees even harder, ignoring the fight or flight instinct that was kicking in. I'd ran once before, back home, but that had been for a reason. My mother. If it came to fight or flight again, I had only once choice. *Fight*. "I'm not running, sir."

"You did it before." For a second, I thought he was referring to me leaving his son all those years ago, and was about to point out the impropriety of mentioning that in a Captain/Detective setting, but then he added: "When you came back here and took a job, you ran from him. Why not do it again?"

"Because I need to stay here."

Ben added, "She's not running. It'll solve nothing. All running gives her is no one to watch her back. She grew up here, has family and friends here. A partner who cares about her and will ensure this never happens to her again. This is where she belongs—with *us*."

"I wouldn't go that far, Detective," his father said, frowning. "There's a bit of animosity in this office for her, as well. She'd be better off with a clean slate in a different state, if you ask me."

Tears blurred my vision, but I blinked them back. Now was not the time. At home alone, in my bed, with the door shut, was the time for me to feel sorry for myself. "I'm not leaving."

"All right, I guess it's my job to keep you safe, then, isn't it?" he said, his tone tinged with resentment over that small fact.

I licked my lips. "Sir, I—"

"It's our duty and our privilege to call her ours, sir," Ben cut in angrily. "And yes, it's our job to help protect one of our own. We'd do it for anyone who works in these walls, or wears a badge, and you can be damned sure I'll do it for the girl I once loved with all my heart."

"We agree on some of that, Detective," he said carefully. Then he turned back to me. "But for me to protect you, I need to ask you some questions. Some personal questions." He glanced at his son briefly. "Would you rather be alone for these inquiries?"

Ben started to stand, clearly thinking he knew my

answer already. I rested a hand on his arm briefly, stopping him. He glanced at me in surprise, our gazes colliding with a force that shook me. "You can stay. Like you said, you're my partner, right?"

"Right," he said.

I broke the eye contact first, taking my hand back and facing my boss before he started to question just how close we'd gotten last night before Ben had told me that. "Ask away, sir."

"Okay." Captain cleared his throat, looking uncomfortable for the first time. "I noticed there are no hospital reports on file."

I said nothing, shaking my head.

"When you say he beat you, I'm just curious what level of violence we're talking about here, so we can better inform the local judges here." He hesitated again, his cheeks reddening. "Slaps? Closed fists? Threats?"

"All of those," I said, regaining my hold on my knees. They were the only thing keeping me grounded right now. "He...hit me, slapped me, choked me, punched me, kicked me, forced himself on me sexually when I tried to refuse him."

Ben cursed under his breath, reaching over and resting a hand on mine, which still clung to my knee. "You don't have to do this."

"Yes, I do," I said hollowly.

Captain kept writing, not looking up.

When he stopped and lifted his head, I swallowed hard, my stomach hollowing out as I relived the drama of my own personal hell. My previous Captain hadn't asked me for details, but clearly that had been because he had no intention of ever actually filing the charges against Vinnie. "The night I finally had enough, he threw me down, climbed on top of me, and choked me until I blacked out. I thought I was going to die. When I didn't, I woke up, crawled toward the door, and reported the abuse. He told me he'd kill me. When I left, I thought he'd be out of my life for good. But... he's not. He's here, and he's going to kill me, just like he promised."

TWENTY

Ben

I was going to kill the son of a bitch.

Some way, somehow, I was going to find him, rip him apart piece by piece, feed him to the ocean, put him back together, and then do it all over again. The things he'd done to Sarah, the atrocities he'd put her through, deserved nothing less. What killed me even more than the pain she'd suffered was the way she recounted it.

He's here, and he's going to kill me, just like he promised.

The way she said it, with no hint of emotion or doubt, sent a chill right down my fucking spine. It was as if she accepted that this was how it was going to end, and there was nothing she could do to avoid it. Well, tough shit. She might think that was the only way this ended, but I didn't agree. I would protect her with my life. Nothing was happening to Sarah Lopez.

Not on *my* watch.

"I'm sorry to put you through this," Captain said, setting his pen down. He swallowed and added, "But we're here for you, and from here on out, I want you guarded at all times."

She stiffened. "That's not necessary, sir. I don't wish to

push undue attention on myself, or apply any undue pressure on my colleagues—whom you yourself have pointed out aren't all that fond of me in the first place."

"Well, I don't wish to have unwanted attention on my precinct when one of my Detectives is killed by a psycho cop from North Carolina." He leaned forward, his face determined. "If you want to allow your partner into your home to help guard your back when you're there, then that's fine. I trust him. But I'm still going to place a rotation of officers outside your home in an unmarked car on a twenty-four-hour basis. Detective Rollins can't live in his car, and continue to carry that load on his own anymore."

She looked at me slowly, her eyes wide.

Well, shit. *Way to blow my cover, Dad.*

"You've been sleeping outside my house?"

I hesitated, then nodded. "On Captain's orders, yes."

"But clearly this will be a long ordeal, until we can A: find this guy, and B: catch him doing something wrong that we can arrest him for, since his record has been expunged." Captain stood. "You can't be the only one outside her house anymore. You need to sleep, and I'd rather you be inside the home, anyway, with someone outside, as well. Understood?"

I nodded, standing also. "Yes, sir."

Sarah fidgeted as she rose to her feet. "With all due respect, sir, isn't that overkill? I'm perfectly capable of taking care—"

"No, it's not. You came here, to my precinct, with this monster chasing after you, so it's my monster now, too, to deal with as I see fit." He took on a defensive stance. "Your partner will help guard the inside, and I'll have an officer outside your home at all times. That's an order. Is that understood, Lopez?"

Sarah stiffened, but nodded, saluting him. "Yes, sir."

"You're excused."

Sarah headed for the door, and I followed her. The second it closed behind us, she spun on me with anger in her eyes. "You've been sleeping in a car outside my house?"

"Yes," I said, keeping my voice down. "Captain's orders."

"Why not just come inside?" She crossed her arms. "Or was that *against* orders?"

"I was given the option of being inside or outside, until now." I cocked a brow. "I chose the latter, clearly."

She pressed her mouth into a line. "Why?"

"Because I knew if I went inside, what happened last night would happen, and I was trying to avoid it, and the complications that it would bring." As soon as the words were out of my mouth, I realized how it sounded, and wanted to take them back. "I mean—"

"Wow." She backed up. Her outward anger did nothing to hide the pain my words had caused her, though. I saw it there, in her deep brown eyes. "Well, sorry to ruin your plans of keeping yourself free of me and my messy complications."

I reached for her hand. "That's not what I meant—"

"Save it. It doesn't matter." She pulled free. "I hope you like my couch. Looks like you'll be spending a lot of time on it."

Okay. She clearly wasn't happy with me. "I can sleep outside if you prefer. The officer can be inside."

She snorted. "And have you defy direct orders? I wouldn't dream of putting you in that position."

"Why are you so pissed?" I asked, glancing over my shoulder. Hernandez watched us, frowning. So did Matthews...and his partner, Rogers. "Is it because I slept outside without telling you, or because you're upset I made you tell Captain the truth about what happened with Vinnie?"

"Both," she hissed. "*Everyone*'s going to know now."

"Who cares? It wasn't your fault. It was his."

"Tell that to everyone in North Carolina who turned on me," she shot back, her voice trembling. "Tell that to my former friends who turned on me, and called me a lying whore that was only seeking attention. You have no idea what it's like to be in this position. *None*."

My heart fisted painfully at the shit she'd gone through. "Sarah—"

"When I came here, I wanted to get a clean slate, away from the man who turned me into something I never want to be again, and away from the judging eyes of people who dared to accuse me of telling the truth for attention. As if someone would want that kind of *attention* on them." She swallowed hard. "But now I'm right back in it, and if you think at least half of those people out there won't judge me and think I'm guilty of lies, then you're fooling yourself."

I searched my mind for the right thing to say, but the truth was I had no clue what that was. It was easy for me to sit here and say that would never happen, that the people in this precinct would never turn on her like that, but who the hell was I to make promises I couldn't keep? I couldn't speak for them, any more than I could speak for her. It was my hope that no one would do that, sure, but I wasn't naïve enough to believe that hopes came true.

They *didn't*.

"If anyone pulls that shit on you, then they'll answer to me," I growled.

She swallowed and swiped her hands down her face. She met my eyes, her own resigned and dull. "I appreciate that, Ben. I really do. But that doesn't change the fact that if

I didn't tell anyone, if I had never opened my mouth and told you the truth, that I wouldn't be here right now, stuck in this situation...*again*."

More eyes were on us now, as we whispered back and forth in the hallway outside Captain's office. I knew we should end this conversation, and finish it later in the privacy of her home, but I'd upset her, and I wasn't about to walk away. "No, you're right. You'd be dead instead, because no one would have your fucking back."

"Hate to break it to you, but guess what?" she shot back. "I'll probably be dead when this is over anyway. You guys can't follow me around for the rest of my life, and he's certainly not going to barge in, and get himself caught. He's too smart for that. All these precautions are a waste of time and department resources. He'll wait it out until your father gives up, and gets comfortable enough to remove the guards, and then when I'm alone, he'll come after me. Putting guys outside my house isn't going to stop him—it'll just delay him."

"Then I guess I'm never leaving your house. I won't give up. I won't get comfortable." I flexed my jaw. "I'm not leaving you until he's gone for good."

She laughed, but it wasn't a real laugh. "Yeah. Sure. Okay. Move in. Live with me for the rest of your life, and give up any chances of ever getting married, and living happily. Dedicate your life to keeping me alive, and protecting me at all costs."

"Gladly," I snapped. "I look forward to it."

"Fine," she shot back sarcastically. "Can't wait."

When I didn't say anything else, she shifted on her feet, looking around nervously. It was then that she must've noticed our audience, because she blanched and stepped back even further from me. "People are watching."

"No shit," I shot back. "We've been arguing for five minutes."

She forced a smile for our crowd, then said, "I'm done here."

"Me too."

Without another word, she stormed off, and I let her, watching her go. As she walked, I followed the gazes of everyone else, and couldn't help but wonder if she was right.

Would they turn on her, once they found out the truth?

TWENTY-ONE

Sarah

———

I tossed pillows, a blanket, and a flat sheet on Ben's lap, not meeting his eyes. "Here you go. You can just leave them out here. I'll wash them when I do my own sheets."

He took them, setting them aside. "You don't have to wash my sheets. I can do them myself."

"My sheets. My laundry. My house." I glanced at his carry-on suitcase, which he'd placed in the corner of the living room. "What's in there?"

"Towels, a couple of sets of clothes, underwear, socks." He turned back to me. "Why? Is that a problem?"

I hugged myself, emotionally drained from everything that had gone on today. Captain had held a meeting with the people assigned to my case, telling only a select few the details of my life and about the man trying to kill me. He'd told them all to keep the details of my case to themselves, and to tell no one...which meant by now, everyone in the precinct knew the whole story.

Couldn't *wait* for work tomorrow.

The truth would come out about who believed me, and

who would hate on me for turning on another cop. "No. It's not a problem. Feel free to hang your stuff in the closet over there so it doesn't wrinkle." I tipped my head toward the coat closet. "Washer's at the end of the hall to the left, and so is the guest bathroom...which you already know. There's a shower in there that you can have to yourself. The other bedroom is my mother's, which is the last door on the right. Don't go in there. She's sleeping and if you wake her up, you'll confuse and upset her."

He nodded. "Okay."

"If you're hungry, you know where the kitchen is. Help yourself to whatever you want. If you empty something, please add it to the list so I can get it when I go shopping."

"When *we* go shopping."

I paused, confused. "Excuse me?"

"If you go shopping, I go, too. You're not going alone. Captain was very clear I'm to be by your side at all times."

I crossed my arms again, anger at this whole situation taking over my life again. Good. It was better than the fear and helplessness that had been nagging me like a long-lost friend I'd hoped to never see again. "Oh. Right. Should I bring you in the ladies' room with me, and the shower, too, to make sure I'm safe in there while I'm washing my hair?"

His lips twitched at the last part. "Well, actually—"

"Oh, shut up," I snapped.

He held his hands up, smiling fully now as he approached me. "You kind of asked for that sort of reply, given the circumstances."

"Just like I asked for you to be here, with me, the night after we had sex and decided it would never happen again?" I tipped my head back so I could stare him down despite the height difference. "Yeah, that sounds like an excellent idea to me."

He flexed his jaw. "I told you I could be the one outside."

"Are you that scared to be close to me?" I taunted, unable to help myself.

After all, he'd frigging slept outside my house without telling me to avoid me. That wasn't exactly the best for my self-esteem, thank you very much.

"I'm not scared of you," he mumbled gruffly.

"Are you sure?" I poked at his chest. "I mean, you wouldn't want to catch my complications. They're contagious—oh, *wait*. Too late. I touched you. You caught them, and look at you now. Stuck here with the girl you just had a one-night stand with."

"Stop it," he snapped, catching my finger.

"Why? Don't like it?" I asked innocently.

"No, I don't fucking *like* it. I shouldn't have said what I said, how I said it, but I slept outside because I didn't want to put you in the position of being stuck with a partner you didn't want, who you'd slept with, and I didn't want to put you at risk for losing your job." He pulled me close. "Those are the complications I meant, not your ex, and protecting you. I'd do that even if we never fucked. I'd do that for a stranger. It's my *job* to keep people safe, Sarah."

I knew that, just like I knew he'd lay his life down for someone he didn't know, without hesitation. It's part of what made him such a great guy. And now here he was, stuck with me, unable to go home, and there was nothing we could do to change it because I'd opened my big fat mouth and told the truth about Vinnie...*again*.

Sometimes, late at night, I wondered if this was all my fault. If I'd invited Vinnie to take advantage of me somehow, and if I could have avoided it if I'd just kept my mouth shut, which was ridiculous. I wasn't at fault, Vinnie was. He was a sick man who needed help, and I couldn't be the one to give it to him. I *knew* all this. But late at night, alone in my bed, my mind went there.

It *always* went there.

"I know it sucks, and I know you're scared, just like I know you're not really angry at me, but more at the world for making this happen to you," Ben said, his tone softening as he loosened his grip on me and pulled me into his arms for a hug. "But please know that being here is not a complication for me. *You're* not a complication. I am here for you, for whatever you need. Always have been. Always will be. That'll never change, no matter how much you take your anger at the world out on me. If you need me to be your punching bag, I'll be your punching bag. If you need me to be your enemy, I'll be that. If you need me to be your friend, I already am. Just ask, and whatever you require is yours. You know that."

He was right. I did.

And just like that, the emotions I'd managed to hold back came flooding to the surface. They broke me, and I curled my face into his chest, clinging to him. I didn't cry, but that didn't mean that I didn't mourn all the things that *should* have been, and all the things that I could have avoided if I'd stayed and fought all those years ago, instead of fleeing.

After all, if I'd done that, if I'd just talked to him instead of leaving like I had, I never would have gone to Duke, and I never would have met Vinnie, and I never would have gone through hell like that.

This was my punishment for breaking his heart.I deserved to be miserable and alone, unable to be with the man that I loved, because I was a horrible person. Part of me was sure this was my penance, that I'd suffer for the rest of my life because I'd jumped to assumptions, and left instead of giving the man who'd always given me everything I asked for a chance to explain himself. *I should have given him a chance to explain himself.*

"I'm sorry," I whispered into his shirt. "I'm so fucking sorry."

"Sh." He cradled the back of my head, smoothing my hair and hugging me close. "I know, babe. I know. Me too."

And then he said nothing else. Just held me.

I looked up at him, and he hesitated before lowering his lips to mine and kissing me. It was undemanding, no strings attached. Just a simple, sweet kiss. When he pulled back, he wiped my tears off my cheeks, pressed my face against his chest again, and held me.

It was perfect...

Just like him.

TWENTY-TWO

Ben

_____

The sun shone through the blinds, and the sound of someone moving around in the kitchen awoke me slowly, but then I startled awake because who the hell was in my kitchen? It took me a few seconds of blinking around the room in confusion to remember where I was, and why I heard someone moving around. I was on Sarah's couch, and it must be her moving around, because she lived here. Yawning, I sat up slowly and rubbed my eyes.

As if she sensed me waking up, she popped her head out of the kitchen. She wore a grey pencil skirt, a button up blouse, and she'd knotted her hair at the back of her neck.

Fucking perfection, like usual.

"How do you like your eggs?" she asked.

"Huh?" I mumbled, still groggy.

"Eggs. Scrambled? Fried?"

"You don't have to cook for me," I said slowly.

She waved the black plastic spatula around. For all intents and purposes, she looked much calmer than the night before. Any hints of vulnerability and fear were gone, and her mouth was relaxed instead of pinched together tightly. "I'm making them for Mom anyway. She's hungry."

"What kind is she having?"

"Scrambled," she replied right away.

"Then scrambled it is."

She nodded. "Go wash up and get ready. It'll be a few minutes."

And then she was gone as quickly as she'd came.

I yawned again, then stood, stretching. I'd slept in a pair of sweats and a loose T-shirt instead of my boxer briefs, since I figured me walking around the house in my underwear wasn't a good idea for either of us. As I made my way barefoot toward the bathroom, I passed her mother's room.

The door was open, and she was sitting up.

I hadn't seen her in years—ten, to be exact. Somerton was a small town by California standards, sure, but that still made it pretty damn big, and I rarely ran into people since I usually spent most of my hours at the precinct.

Her hair was grayer than I remembered, and someone had brushed it smoothly over her shoulders, more than likely Sarah. She wore a nightgown with flowers on it, and was tucked in cozily with knitting on her lap. I'd read a study once that Alzheimer's patients retained memories of activities that required hand eye coordination, even though they couldn't remember the year, or their names. Guess that held true, since she was knitting *some*thing.

As if she sensed me standing there, she lifted her head and looked at me. Frowning, she cocked her head. "Who's there?"

I started to back up, remembering quite well that Sarah ordered me to leave her alone so I didn't upset her.

But then she ordered, "Come in, young man."

Hesitating, I glanced over my shoulder, then stepped

forward. It wasn't in my DNA to disobey a direct order, especially not from a sick old woman. "Yes, Mrs. Lopez?"

"Who are you?" She studied me. I stood a little straighter. "Are you new here? I don't remember seeing you before, and yet...you remind me of someone."

I stepped closer, smiling. "I'm new, but I've been here a few times. How are you feeling today, Mrs. Lopez?"

"Tired." She yawned. "The other nurse is making me eggs. Are they almost ready?"

The other nurse... Sarah? She didn't know who her own daughter was? Well, shit. I mean, yeah, I kind of knew that, but seeing it first hand was different. "They'll be ready soon."

"Excellent." She winced. "Can you adjust my pillows? My back hurts."

"Of course." I went inside the room, my steps slow. Should I fix them, or let Sarah handle it? Was there a proper way to do so? I was way outta my league here, and I knew it. "Did you sleep well last night, Mrs. Lopez?"

"I did." She sat up, saying nothing more.

I reached around her gingerly, hesitated, then squeezed the pillow directly behind her, fluffing it up. After doing the same to the rest of them, I smiled and said, "All set."

She leaned back, sighing. "Perfect, thank you." She glanced at the window. "Can we go for a walk today? The sun is shining."

I glanced outside, too. It was, indeed, shining...but I wasn't sure if she could go on walks. Her brain wasn't functioning properly, sure, but what about the rest of her? Was she allowed outside with supervision? I made a mental note to ask Sarah for more information on her mother, so if this happened again I'd feel less like a fish out of water. "I'll have to ask the other nurse. I'm too new to answer that."

"All right," she said, her tone dismissive.

I backed toward the door. "If that's all—"

"Can you find my yarn?"

I swallowed hard, glancing over my shoulder. Where the hell was Sarah? "Your yarn?"

"Yes, it's red. I'm making my baby a hat."

"Your...baby?" I said slowly, walking toward her. "You mean Sarah?"

She lit up. "Yes. You've seen her? Isn't she adorable?"

"She is." I swallowed hard and lifted the red yarn and needles off her lap. It was, indeed, what looked to be a baby hat. My heart wrenched, both for the woman in the bed and for Sarah. "The cutest."

Mrs. Lopez took the yarn. "She takes after me."

"Of course."

"Do you know how to knit?" she asked me.

"Actually, yes, I do." I perched on the edge of the bed. "My mother taught me when I was eleven. I never stopped, and still occasionally pick up the needles to relax. It's been too long since I held some yarn, though. I'll have to start a project."

"How long?"

"Months," I admitted. "Almost a year."

She beamed. "No one should go that long without knitting in their lives. Want to do a few stitches for my baby?"

"I..." I hesitated. "Are you sure? It's your project."

"I'm sure." She held it out again. "Go on."

I took it, positioning the ball of yarn in my lap. I studied the pattern. Standard ribbing: purl two, knit two. "This looks great."

"Thank you."

I slid the needle inside the yarn. "How old is your baby?"

"Six months." She lit up even more. "She rolls over, and is almost crawling already. She's so terribly clever."

"Indeed." I slid the stitch to the other needle. "I'm a huge fan of your daughter's."

Mrs. Lopez studied him. "Are you?"

"I am."

She touched his hand. "Don't forget to switch to the knit stitch."

"I won't." I did as told.

"Do you sing?"

I blinked. "Excuse me?"

"Do you sing? Your voice..." She faded off, staring into the distance.

After a period of silence, I swallowed. "I sing in the car, and the shower, when I'm alone."

"Can you sing for me?"

Well, shit. I'd never sung in front of someone before. "What song?"

"Anything."

I racked my brain for a song I could sing, and settled on a song I'd heard on the radio yesterday by Ed Sheeran. I sang to her, low and soft, as I knit. She laid back on the pillows, closing her eyes and smiling. I watched her as I knit and sang to her, my heart wrenching painfully in my chest. This woman, this vibrant woman, had lost so much in her life...

But so had *Sarah*.

She'd come back here, despite the risks to herself, to care for a mother who no longer remembered who she was. It was a horrible reality to have to face daily—all alone. I kept singing, keeping my voice soft as I started a new row. She'd closed her eyes, and she looked at peace, so I didn't want to stop.

"Your eggs are ready, Mrs.—" Sarah came into the room, breaking off midsentence. She stared at me with wide eyes, her face going pale, and her gaze dipped to the knit hat in my hands. "What are you doing?"

I stopped singing immediately, standing with a pounding heart. "I...uh..."

"Sit again, please," Mrs. Lopez said, catching my hand. "Keep singing to me."

Sarah stared even harder now, her grip on the tray of food tight. "*Singing?*"

"She asked me to sing to her and knit," I said gently, standing up despite her mother's pleas. "So I did."

She said nothing. Just *stared*.

Turning my back on her, I set the knitting down in her mother's lap. Smiling, I leaned down to her level and touched her cheek gently. "I'll sing to you again later, okay? Eat your eggs now."

Her mother nodded. "I am hungry."

Sarah pulled herself together and passed him with the tray. "They're nice and hot, just the way you like them."

"Did you make some for my baby?"

Sarah forced a smile as she set the tray down. I knew I should go, but I felt like she needed someone there with her. "Yes, she's eating now."

Grace came in, wearing a pair of green scrubs. "Sorry I'm late. I hit traffic, but I'm here now. Go get ready, I'll stay in here with her."

"It's okay." Sarah didn't look his way. "Come on, Ben. Breakfast is ready."

As we walked away, I heard Mrs. Lopez ask, "Can you sing to me while I eat? That other nurse had such a nice voice."

I swallowed and closed the door behind us. The second

we were alone, I started talking. Knowing Sarah, she was pissed as hell at me for intruding on her personal life like that. "I was walking by, and she spotted me. I swear that I didn't upset her, I just followed her—"

Whatever I'd been about to say got cut off as Sarah pushed me against the wall, slammed her body against mine, and kissed me. It was the first time she'd willingly done so since we'd been thrown back together, and there was something behind it—an emotion I couldn't name—that took my damn breath away.

Groaning, I caught the back of her shirt at the base of her spine, fisting it and pulling her against my chest. Her mouth opened, and I took full advantage of that, sweeping my tongue into her mouth without even a hint of hesitation even though this shouldn't be happening right now.

If Captain found out...

Hating myself for caring, I pulled back and ended the kiss before things went too far. She immediately went in for another kiss, making a protesting sound as she buried her hands in my hair and tugged me down.

I resisted. "Sarah..."

She froze at the sound of my voice. She looked up at me —confusion, need, and pain in those deep dark brown depths of hers—not moving. I could see it. The desire to keep going, despite the consequences. I wish I could feel the same, but I couldn't do that to her.

There was too much on the line.

"I want this. I want you." I swallowed. "But we can't. If we get caught by—"

She pushed off me, pushing her hair out of her face. "I know."

"Sarah—"

She held a shaking hand up. "*I know.*"

Without another word, she headed for the kitchen. I followed her, my body aching to stop her, spin her in my arms, and take her against the wall until we both forgot every single reason we shouldn't be together...

No matter the cost.

TWENTY-THREE

Sarah

———

"*E*xcuse me, are you Sarah?" an unfamiliar masculine voice said from behind me. It was shortly after lunch, and the police station was buzzing with activity. People talked all around me, the low murmur of voices somehow becoming a calming sound to my strung-out nerves.

I turned on my heel, exhaustion taking over me and making my reflexes slower. Knowing that Vinnie was out there somewhere watching me didn't exactly help me get a good night's rest...and neither did having my only other ex under my roof. "Yes?"

"Delivery." The messenger held out a handheld device. "Sign here, please?"

"Who from?" I asked, carefully examining the small envelope in his hand.

"It says..." He squinted. "Anonymous."

Vinnie. My stomach fisted. "Do I have to accept it?"

"Well, no..."

I sensed who was behind me before he even spoke.

"What's this?" Ben asked, stopping just short of pressing his shoulder to mine.

"An anonymous delivery," I said, not bothering to tell him to mind his own business. For now, he was all up in mine, and there was nothing I could do to change that.

This morning...with my mother...

He'd gotten past defenses I'd had in place for ten years now, and because he had, there was no way I was going to be able to put them back in place. He'd knocked down walls, and they weren't going back up. If he hadn't stopped that kiss this morning, nothing would have stopped me from bringing him in my room to find out if he was as good as I remembered or not.

Not even the threat of losing my *job*.

"Sign for it."

Sighing, I did as he said, and took the envelope.

"Come on," he said, heading for his father's office.

I followed him silently, not wanting to see what was inside, yet knowing I had to. He held the door open for me, and I walked inside. He shut it behind both of us, and his father was there, waiting behind his desk. "Sir, Sarah got an anonymous delivery."

The captain sat up straighter, picked up his phone, and called someone. "Hello, send Thomas in. I have something he needs to check." He hung up and motioned us forward. "Forensics is on its way. Bring it here."

Ben walked forward. I stayed where I was.

"Is it from him?"

I shrugged. "I haven't opened it, sir."

"Well, let's do so." He pulled a pair of latex gloves out of the box behind him, and opened it gingerly. I crept forward, my heart pounding hard. As he slid the single piece of paper out, I held my breath. "It says... 'I'm coming.'"

"What?" I asked, letting out the breath.

"That's it. 'I'm coming.'"

Sounded like Vinnie. He liked to keep his threats low-key.

More effective that way.

Ben snarled. "Asshole."

"We'll dust it for fingerprints." He carefully slid it back in the envelope, then set it down. "Any activity at the house last night?"

I avoided Ben's eyes. "No, sir."

"I didn't hear anything," Ben agreed. "Neither did the uniform outside the house."

"Were you inside?" he asked.

"Yes."

I added, "On the couch, sir."

He eyed me. "I figured."

"Just making sure. I'd hate to lose my job."

"You're aware of what would happen if you crossed that line." He turned to his son. "You both are. I trust you to follow the rules, and not risk termination."

"Sir—" Ben started stiffly.

"We're not discussing the rules that you both agreed to when you accepted a job in this office. You signed the contract, and the rules stand." He rested his hands on the top of his desk. "We are discussing Detective Lopez's safety. Will you continue to sleep in the house, or is there a problem with that?"

"There's no problem," Ben gritted out.

"Then keep on as you have. We'll dust this for fingerprints, but I'm sure he covered his tracks. He's a cop, after all."

Ben nodded and headed for the door.

"I have a question, sir," I said quietly.

His father nodded. "All right. Go on."

I glanced at Ben, who had stopped walking. "I'd like to ask it...alone."

Ben's shoulders stiffened.

"You're dismissed, Detective," Captain said.

Ben walked out, saying nothing.

As soon as the door shut, Captain frowned at me. "What's up?"

"I was wondering if it might be possible for me to get reassigned to a new partner?"

He crossed his arms. "Has Detective Rollins done something wrong?"

"No, he's a great partner."

He cocked a brow. He looked so much like his son in that moment that it was almost freaky. "Then why get a new one?"

"You know why, sir."

He snorted. "The pairing stays."

"I understand you don't like me, sir, and I'm not trying to change that, but—"

"But nothing. I paired the two of you up because the rookie cop you spoke of who needed an established detective to learn from. You did, too. It had nothing to do with whether I liked you or not."

I stepped closer. "You're setting us up for failure, sir."

"If you fail, you have no one to blame but yourselves. You're not children. You know the rules, and I expect you to follow them."

I opened my mouth. "And if we don't?"

"Then you'll both be looking for a new job."

He did this on purpose. Put us together so he didn't have to worry about me catching his son in my grasp again. He knew it. Ben knew it. So did I. But there was no way to prove it, so unless I wanted to go to war with my new boss, there wasn't anything I could do about it. I needed this job, and the medical insurance, so guess what? I kept my mouth shut.

I headed for the door. When my hand was on the knob, he called out, "Detective Lopez?"

"Yes, sir?" I asked without turning around.

"You're right. I don't like you very much. When you left my son behind, you broke him in ways I've never seen. I don't trust you. I didn't want to hire you." He let out a breath. "But I did, and I am going to protect you. Play it safe, and don't force me to do something I have no intention of doing. I happen to like your mother very much."

I stiffened, facing him. "What does my mother have to do with this?"

"She's a dependent on your paperwork. I'm aware you're caring for her, and believe it or not, after you left town, we kept in touch. I'm fully aware of her medical condition, and it was the only reason I allowed the precinct to force you upon us." He flexed his jaw. "Don't jeopardize her care for a little bit of rebellion with my son for old time's sake. It's not worth it."

I swallowed hard. "Yes, sir."

Without saying anything else, I left his office. As I stepped into the hallway, Ben was there, leaning against the wall with his ankles crossed as tightly as his arms. "Good?"

I nodded, not meeting his gaze. "Yep."

"Let me guess. You asked for a new partner, and got denied."

"Does it matter?" I shot back.

I walked past him, but he caught my arm, halting me.

"Kind of." His grip on me shifted. "I thought we were getting along."

"That's precisely the problem, now isn't it?" I locked gazes with him. "We're getting along a little too well, and even though I keep telling myself to keep my distance, to not push my luck, I know, deep down that if you let me, I'd lose it all for you, and I can't do that to my mother."

He swallowed hard, his grip on me loosening. "Sarah..."

"Don't. Just don't."

Letting go of me, he swallowed and stepped back. He'd put the distance between us that I didn't have the strength to find. "I would never let you lose it all."

"I know, because you're that good of a guy, which only makes it worse. This would be so much easier if you were the asshole I spent these last ten years thinking you were." I closed my eyes for a second, then added with brutal honesty, "I wish you'd cheated on me. I wish you were every inch the bastard I thought you were, because this would be *so* much easier."

And with that?

I walked away.

TWENTY-FOUR

Ben

I woke up to the sound of something hitting wood. What kind of wood, what kind of object, I had no fucking clue. But it had woke me up, and I wasn't about to ignore the instinct that told me something was going on. Rolling off the couch in one smooth motion, I grabbed my gun and tiptoed toward the front door, barefoot and only wearing a pair of sweats. The hair on the back of my neck rose, and every nerve in my body heightened with awareness.

If that asshole was out there, lurking in Sarah's bushes, I didn't care if we were lacking proof of his treachery—he'd be a dead man without that proof. He wasn't going to touch a damn hair on Sarah's head.

As I crept closer to the door, Sarah moaned in her room, followed by that same *thunk*ing noise against wood. Switching direction, I hurried toward her room as quietly as I could. If he was in her room...

I turned the knob slowly, making sure to keep it silent. A situation like this called for silent stealth—not forced entry. That knocking sound happened again, as I slid the door open and crept inside. I searched for signs of another man, for an intruder, but came up empty.

She moaned again, and my attention slammed into her on the bed, writhing...with her hand between her legs. Her eyes were closed, and she bit her lip to keep quiet, but it wasn't working. I heard every sound she made.

Every. Fucking. Sound.

I told myself not to move. Told myself to turn around, close that door, and pretend I hadn't just witnessed the most erotic thing I've ever seen in my life. Told myself to forget it ever happened, because I was a good guy, and good guys didn't take advantage of women when they weren't supposed to. I even took a step backward, into the hallway, but then...*then* she said the one word guaranteed to make me stop dead in my tracks.

One simple word.

"Ben..."

My attention snapped to her face. At first, I thought she saw me, but her eyes hadn't opened, and her hand was moving faster now. Harder. Her breath came faster, and her breasts rose and fell as she writhed on the bed, letting her legs open more, and I'm going to be honest here. Nothing, I repeat, *nothing*, would have stopped me from doing what came next.

Growling, I shut the door, locked it, and laid my gun on her dresser. I stalked across the room, no longer bothering to be quiet. Her eyes flew open, and she stared at me, cheeks flushed in the moonlight, her hand still between her thighs. Seeing her fingers on herself, over that sexy strip of satin she called panties, was enough to make me forget all about being a good guy.

I climbed on top of her, laid my body on hers, and kissed her with all the pent-up frustration I'd been feeling since the last time we'd slipped. Her smooth skin touched mine, and I ran my hands over her body, touching everywhere I could find. Her hips. Her ass. Her thighs.

When I slid my hand between us, covering her fingers but not actually touching her, she gasped into my mouth and started moving her hand again. She circled her clit, rubbing hard, her breath coming fast as her tongue swirled around mine. Every stroke, every touch, brought her higher until her whole body stiffened beneath mine, and she came with my name on her lips. "*Ben.*"

Without waiting a second more, I rolled onto my back and slid my hands down my sweats, closing my fist over my hard cock. She got on her knees, eyes wide as I jerked, staring at her as my hand slid up and down my shaft. She bit her lip and let out the sexiest moan I'd ever heard, climbed on top of me, and rode me as my hand moved over myself, giving me the sexiest lap dance I'd ever had. Her ass brushed the tip of my cock as I jerked off, the satin panties, sweats and shred of self-control the only thing that kept me from rolling her over and fucking her properly.

She kissed me, her soft lips on mine as she slid her core against me, teasing me and driving me closer to the edge with every thrust. When she trailed her fingers down my chest and over my abs, I thrust into my hand, so close I could taste it almost as clearly as I tasted her. She slipped her hand inside my sweats, covering my hand with hers like I'd done to her, and held on.

Her fingers on my skin as I touched myself was exactly what I needed to come. I threaded my hand through her hair, deepened the kiss, and came in an explosion of fireworks.

That's right. Motherfucking fireworks.

I collapsed on her pillows, trying to catch my breath,

and she rolled off me, hugging herself as she knelt there, staring at me. We studied one another, neither of us daring to speak because we'd crossed the line again, and we both knew it. We might not have fucked, but we might as well have.

Still. We *hadn't*.

Her lips twitched slightly, and her smile broke the silence. "You always were good at finding ways around the rules."

I rubbed my face with both hands, staring at the ceiling fan whirring overhead with a soft buzzing sound. "I know. I'm sorry. I just...I thought you were in trouble, heard some banging."

She snorted.

"Jesus," I grunted, smiling despite myself. "Grow up."

"Never," she vowed.

"*Any*way." I reached out and tugged on a piece of her hair playfully, because who the hell was I kidding? I'd never grown up, either, and had no intention of ever doing so. "I heard noises, and thought you were under attack, so I came in with my gun—"

Her jaw dropped.

"—but you were alone, and then you said my name..."

Her cheeks flushed, and she slammed her mouth shut. "Oh, God. I did?"

"You did."

She flopped onto her back dramatically. "Get that gun, and shoot me now."

"Never." I rolled onto my side, propping myself up on my elbow. I reached out slowly and touched her soft cheek, brushing my knuckles against it tenderly. "I'll never hurt you, Sarah, and that's why I'm going to walk out that door, and as far as I'm concerned, that was a hot dream I had. This never happened, and we didn't toe the line tonight."

She swallowed. "We can't keep doing this."

"I know. There's too much on the line right now." I pulled my touch away. "It won't happen again."

Wincing, she looked at me with an honesty in her eyes that was impossible to ignore. "I know, and that's what scares me the most. I wish…"

"I know." I forced a smile as I stood. "Me too."

"Did you ever ask for a new partner?"

"Repeatedly. He refused." I stood and rubbed the back of my neck. My sweats were sticking to me, and I needed a shower and a change of clothes before they dried to my skin. "He wants us together so we can't be together."

She swallowed. "I figured. I'm sorry he threw you in with me just to keep you away from me."

"There's nothing to be sorry for."

She shook her head. "Sure there is. You're forced to stay here, and not go home, all because my ex—"

"Haven't you learned by now, Sarah?" I smiled again, leaning down and kissing her sweaty forehead. "I'm not forced into doing shit when it comes to you, because I'd do anything for you."

That was the truth.

I headed for the door, not looking back, because if I looked back, I wouldn't leave her in that bed alone. I'd crawl back inside it, climb on top of her, and show her just how much I'd do for her, if given the chance. Instead, I grabbed my gun, tiptoed past her mother's door, and went into the bathroom. As I turned the water on, I stepped out of my dirty sweats and climbed into the shower naked. My body was still humming with desire and it was in no way satisfied with my hand. I still needed her, but I couldn't have her.

Resting my forehead on the cool tile, I closed my fist over my cock and closed my eyes, picturing her lying on her bed with her hand between her thighs and my name on her lips, pleasure deepening her voice as she cried out to me. My hand tightened, and I jerked harder, refusing to stop until I came again, since I wouldn't be sleeping until I did. I bit my tongue, refusing to cry out in case she heard me, and I put us back into the situation we'd been in moments before.

My abs flexed as I closed my eyes, picturing her naked body in my mind, and the way the goosebumps rose over her flesh before she came. In my head, her nipples were hard, begging for my touch, and as her hand slid between her thighs, my mouth was right there, ready and willing to help in ways I hadn't let myself help earlier. As my mouth closed over her, she cried out and writhed beneath me, closing her thighs on either side of my head. In my head, we were together, and she brought me to heights I'd never seen before.

My hand moved faster, and in my mind's eye it was her hand on me, not my own. She closed her mouth over me, taking me in between her lush lips, and I was a goner. I came with her name on my tongue, biting it back so I didn't make a sound, the cool tile against my blazing skin the only reminder that what had just happened wasn't real.

It had all been a fantasy.

But in my mind, in that fantasy, nothing stood in the way of me having her. She was mine. I was hers. Having that feeling inside me—real or not—only showed me that I was right. One way or another, after this was all over, I had to find a way to make this fantasy into a reality.

She *had* to be mine again.

TWENTY-FIVE

Sarah

$\mathcal{I}$ sat at the table, blinking as the conversation carried on around me with ease. Ben had dragged me out for dinner with his friends, one of which was Hernandez—who I clearly knew very well, since we worked together. The others—Carrie, Finn, Riley, and Noelle—I'd never met before, but they seemed friendly enough. The four I'd just met were all married, and very happily so, from what I could tell. Noelle and Riley had been stealing kisses all night, and Carrie and Finn were just as enthusiastically hanging on one another.

That left me, Ben, and Hernandez as the odd men out.

Finn, a man with tattoos up his arms and sandy blond hair, leaned closer to me and said, "How's it feel, coming back home after being on the east coast?"

"Weird," I admitted. "Californians are so different from the people over there."

He nodded. "I know. They're actually polite on the east coast."

I choked on a laugh. "Are you from there originally?"

"Kinda." He shrugged. "I was a kid in Cali, but then my

dad got a job on security for Carrie's father in DC, so I spent most of my life there, until she moved out here for college."

"And you two went to the same school?"

"Not exactly," he said dryly.

Riley piped in from across the table. Clearly, he'd been listening in on our conversation. "He was her secret guard. He watched over her without her knowing it. They ended up falling in love, and then she found out the truth and told him to kiss her ass."

My eyes went wide. "Seriously?"

Carrie, a beautiful redhead with bright blue eyes, crossed her arms. "Seriously."

"Clearly, we worked through it." Finn threw his arm around her shoulders. "Right, babe?"

She pursed her lips, snuggling against him despite her: "*Hmph.*"

"And you two?" I asked, smiling at Noelle, who was the quietest of them all. "What's your story?"

"We met in a hotel bar, and she brought my drunk ass to her room out of pity since they were all booked up." Riley grinned. "Something I took full advantage of."

She pushed her husband playfully. "Hush, you."

"Sounds pretty normal," I said, picking up my drink and taking a swig.

"It was...until I left her money on the dresser, and she thought I thought she was a hooker, and it all went crazy from there on out."

I choked on my beer.

Finn burst into laughter.

Carrie smacked his arm.

"Ow," he said, glaring at her.

Hernandez grinned. "I remember that."

"We *all* do," Noelle shot back, scowling at her husband.

I looked at Hernandez. "And you?"

"Uh…" He raised a brow. "What about me?"

"How do you fit into this little group?"

"I was in the military with Finn. When he went overseas, I took over his bodyguard duties with Carrie. Then, later when I decided on a career change I went to college, met Ben—and the rest is history."

"But…" I gestured at the other people. "No great love stories like theirs?"

Hernandez stiffened. "Nope."

"Actually—" Carrie started.

"I said nope."

Finn rolled his eyes. "Whatever, man."

"Who is she?" I asked, focusing on Ben since he was the most likely to spill his guts.

Ben sighed. "Carrie's old roommate. Marie."

Hernandez shot the middle finger his way.

"They had a thing for one another, but nothing ever happened," Carrie explained. "Just lots of tension and awkward silences that still continue to this day when they see one another."

I frowned. "Is she married?"

"No."

"Dating someone seriously?" I asked again.

Finn shook his head. "Not right now, anyway."

I looked at Hernandez. "So why is she just a story, and not sitting here with us?"

"Because she isn't a story, or anything else. She's just an old acquaintance," Hernandez said, his mouth pinched tight. "These guys just want to pair us off to complete the circle."

Ben lifted his beer. "Bullshit."

"It's not bullshit. There's nothing between me and Marie. Never has been." Hernandez turned his attention on Ben, and I stiffened, knowing what was coming next. "Speaking of which...why don't you tell them *your* story?"

"Fuck off," Ben shot back.

Finn leaned forward. "Do tell. The girls would love to hear it."

"The girls can speak for themselves," Carrie muttered to him.

"I know. But we know you want to know," Finn argued.

"I would," Carrie said. "But still."

Noelle perked up for the first time that night. "There's a story?"

"There's always a story," Riley said, grinning.

Ben flexed his jaw, staring straight ahead.

I found my napkin suddenly very interesting.

"They used to be high school sweethearts," Hernandez said, since we weren't about to. "Were happy as could be, until one day Sarah decided to up and move across the country without telling him why."

"Oh shit, this is *her*?" Finn asked.

"*Shh*," Riley hissed.

Oh God, they'd talked about me?

Noelle looked from Ben, to me, and back again. "But... Why?"

"Yeah, *why*?" Hernandez said, grinning at me.

"Because I'm an asshole," I said.

At the same time, Ben said, "She thought she saw me in my bed with another girl."

"What?" Hernandez said.

Carrie's eyes widened.

"*Ben*," I hissed.

"We might as well tell them the truth," he said, shrugging. "They're not going to give up until we do. Besides, we have nothing to hide."

I sagged in my chair.

He continued: "I let a buddy use my bed, and when she went in and saw who she thought was me in the bed with someone else, she lost it, packed up, and accepted an offer at Duke. The rest was history, till she came back and our captain partnered us up."

Finn whistled through his teeth. "So, all this time, you thought he cheated on you..."

"And you thought she left you for no reason," Noelle said with wonder. "I need to write this down. Give me a pen, Riley."

I blinked at her. "Excuse me?"

"Sorry." She took the pen from Riley. "I write romance."

"And Riley writes mysteries," Carrie added, smiling.

"O-Oh. Cool."

She wiggled it in the air. "Do you mind?"

I shook my head.

Ben waved a hand at her. "Do what you must."

"So, what's it like now?" Carrie asked, watching her closely. *Too* closely. "How is it working together with all that history?"

"It's good," Ben said.

"Fine," I added.

We looked at one another.

Finn cleared his throat. "Wow."

"Yeah." Ben turned away first. "Wow."

Noelle finished writing, and bit her lip. "Why did he partner the two of you up in the first place? Just bad luck?"

"Something like that."

Ben snorted.

"So he hates you both?" Carrie asked.

"Something like that," I muttered again. "Though, really, just me."

"Their captain is Ben's father, remember?" Finn said to Carrie.

"Ooooh, that's right."

Noelle lifted her head and gasped. "Let me guess, there's a strict anti-fraternization rule in the precinct?"

Ben pointed at her. "Correct."

Noelle picked up her pen and started writing again.

I groaned. My life was about to become the plot of her next bestseller. Inside the pages of Noelle's book, her story would end happily. I couldn't help but wonder...would *mine*?

"Change of subject?" Ben interjected, shooting me an apologetic grin. "How *is* Marie, Carrie?"

"She's great. She asked about you the other day."

I stiffened.

Hernandez glowered.

"Oh yeah?" Ben asked, seemingly unaware of both those things. "What she say?"

"Actually, she asked if you were still single." She shrugged, side-eying Hernandez. "She has a thing for cops."

Ben grinned and rubbed his stomach. "Hell yeah, she does. Last time we saw one another at your Halloween party—"

"I'm getting a drink. Anyone want one?" Hernandez shot in gruffly.

I raised a hand. "Me."

"Me too," Ben said.

"Fuck off," his best friend shot back.

Carrie gasped.

Finn laughed.

Hernandez walked away.

Ben sighed dramatically.

"Why do you do that to him?" Riley asked.

"Because I'm sick of them both being stupid and stubborn." She leaned back in the chair and took a sip of her Coke. "They need to just hook up already, and put all of us out of our misery."

"I know," Ben agreed.

I still sat stiffly.

"Nothing happened between me and Marie," Ben said under his breath.

"Whatever."

Carrie glanced at me and smiled. "She didn't really ask if he was single, Sarah. Relax."

"I am relaxed," I said immediately. "Why wouldn't I be relaxed?"

Finn snorted.

Carrie elbowed him.

Noelle kept writing.

Riley rubbed her back and watched as she wrote.

"Welcome to the group, Sarah," Ben said dryly.

They all smiled at me, even Noelle, and I couldn't help but think...

What had I gotten myself into?

TWENTY-SIX

Ben

_____

*S*arah was smiling. Actually *smiling*. It had been a while since I'd seen her look happy, or carefree, and I had to admit it...if that had anything to do with me, then I was going to smile, too. She'd balked at the idea of going out with me and my friends, but in the end, we'd all gotten along splendidly, just as I'd suspected we would. After all, Sarah was incredible.

Just as amazing as my friends.

There was no denying that there were feelings still there between us—real, undeniable, strong ones. But in our current situation, no matter how much I might wish it were different, I wasn't free to pursue those feelings. The punishment wasn't worth the risk. I wouldn't be the reason Sarah Lopez lost her job...

Or her ability to care for her mother.

She unlocked the door and smiled over her shoulder at me. Her brown hair fell in soft waves down her back, and she had on one of those skirts that hugged her ass and begged for me to—no, I was going to stop that thought right there. Nothing about her body begged for me to do anything. "Guess what?"

I snapped out of my thoughts. "What?"

"I had fun tonight. Thanks for insisting I go out. It's been a while since I hung out with a group of friends like that."

"How long?" I asked out of curiosity, holding the screen door open for her.

"Since before Vinnie. He didn't like me going out...or having friends."

I swallowed hard. "Asshole."

"Yeah." She walked inside, and I followed her. "Being home, with you, it's brought out a side of me that I thought had died. The kind that actually knows how to socialize, and laugh..."

I closed the door and forced my hands to stay at my side, even though my fingers itched to reach out and touch her soft cheek. To comfort her. "I'm sorry that happened to you, and even sorrier I wasn't there to help."

"I left you, remember?" she said quietly. "If I hadn't—"

"Don't go there."

She bit her lower lip. "How can I not?"

"Sarah..." I said, stepping closer to her, my arm outstretched.

Someone cleared their throat behind us, and she jumped slightly.

My hand dropped back to my side where it belonged.

"How was dinner?" Grace asked, watching us with an expressionless expression.

"Great," Sarah said, tucking her hair behind her ear. "How's Mom?"

"She's still awake. She told me she was waiting up for

the 'male nurse who sings and knits' to come in." Grace glanced at me. "I'm assuming that's you?"

"Y-Yeah," I said slowly.

"She *remembers* him?"

I knew immediately what she was thinking.

Her own mother had forgotten her, but she remembered some guy who visited her the other morning and never came back in? Little did she know, though, I had. I'd made a habit of visiting Mrs. Lopez every day. She liked when I knitted her hats, and sang Ed Sheeran songs to her, so I did it daily. My voice calmed her, and she often fell asleep while I sang. It seemed like it was the least I could do while living under Sarah's roof.

"Apparently," Grace said.

Sarah swallowed.

Something twisted in my chest. "Sarah—"

"It's fine. It's good. I'm happy she likes you." She wrapped her arms around herself. "Do you mind—?"

"Of course not," I said immediately. "I'll go in now."

She caught my hand as I passed. "Ben?"

"Yes?"

"Thank you."

I squeezed her hand. "Nothing to thank me for, Sar."

She let me go, and I made my way back to her mom's room, my heart pounding hard for more reasons than one. I hadn't called her by her nickname since we'd been together, and it had felt...right. I hadn't really known where we might go after we took care of this whole ex-boyfriend thing, but I had a vision in my head now—and it didn't include us being platonic partners. After we put that asshole behind bars where he belonged?

It would be time to get my girl back.

If I had to leave my father's precinct to make it happen,

then so be it. I'd lived a life without Sarah, and I'd lived a life with her at my side, and I could tell you, without a doubt, that I preferred the latter. If she felt the same way as me, I'd do anything, sacrifice *anything*, to have her again.

Walking into the room, I pasted a smile on. "Mrs. Lopez. You shouldn't have waited up for me. It's late."

"Not too late for me," she said, smiling at me. She fumbled in her lap for her knitting, which was where it always was, and handed it off to me. "Do you mind?"

She sounded so much like her daughter in that moment that it physically hurt. "Of course not."

"You started a new one?"

She flushed. "I did. Pink this time. Sarah loves pink."

Sarah *hated* pink. "Yes, she does."

Sarah slid inside the room, arching a brow at me. I knew what she asked. She wanted to know if it was okay if she stayed. I never sang in front of her before, and to be honest, that made me a little nervous, but at the same time, it felt like something she should see. Her mother at ease like this. I nodded at her, then focused on her mother, pretending she wasn't there.

It was best that way.

"Did you bind off the other hat?" I asked.

"I did." She smiled. "It's there."

She motioned to the right. There was a pile of baby hats. I wondered idly what Sarah did with them all. "Nice."

"Sing to me?" She yawned, covering her mouth. Despite her bravado, it was late, and she was tired. By the end of the song, she'd more than likely be asleep.

"Any requests?" I asked teasingly, knitting.

"The one about him loving the girl till they're old."

That could be a handful of Ed Sheeran songs, but I went with the one that fit best. Swallowing hard, I glanced at Sarah, who leaned against the corner watching me, and then focused on her mother again. *She's not there. Not listening.*

I sang to Mrs. Lopez, keeping my voice pleasantly low, working my way through the whole song. Her eyes started to drift shut, so I started over, knowing from experience if I changed songs it would jar her awake. As her breathing evened out, and her face relaxed, I tucked her in, knowing she was sound asleep and would remain that way for the evening.

Then, and only then, I glanced at Sarah.

She watched me, her hand pressed to her mouth, tears running down her cheeks. She looked so beautiful standing there, overcome with emotion, and try as I might, I couldn't break eye contact. I continued singing, but at some point, my song stopped being for her mother, and became a song for her. A *promise* to the girl I used to love, and the woman she'd become.

Setting the knitting aside, I crossed the room, singing the last words as I closed the distance between us. As I finished, she took a shuddering breath, dropping her hand from her mouth. Trembling, she offered it to me, and I took it without hesitation. She led me out in the hallway, and I quietly closed the door behind us. All the lights in the house were off, so I could only assume we were alone. "Grace?" I asked.

"Gone," she said. We stood in the hallway, silence and darkness surrounding us. "Do you do that often? Sing her to sleep?" she asked, her voice thick with emotion.

I nodded, then remembered she couldn't see me. "Yes. I hope you don't mind."

"I don't." A brief silence. "And the knitting?"

"Yeah, that, too."

"I donate the hats to Somerton Hospital. They give them to babies and sick kids..." She shifted closer to me. I couldn't see her, but I could sense it. "She just keeps knitting them for no one."

"Not no one." I reached through the darkness, searching out and finding her cheek. "You."

"Baby me. Not me." She swallowed and leaned into my hand. "She likes you."

"I like her, too."

Silence, and then: "I like you."

"I..." My heart sped up and I flexed my jaw. "I like you, too."

Without warning, she closed the distance between us, rose on her tiptoes, and pressed her mouth to mine. I knew I should stop. Knew this was bad. Yet...I could no sooner stop breathing.

Gripping her hips, I kissed her back, my heart thudding against my ribs. Something broke through my subconscious —a bang, or a creak of the house—and I jerked away. "Sarah—"

"I know we shouldn't, and I know we can't be together, but seeing you with my mom like that..." She swallowed and tightened her grip on me. "I don't care anymore. About any of it. Right here, right now, in the dark... I need you, Ben. I have made a habit to not need anyone, to never need anyone again, but I'm telling you... *I need you*."

TWENTY-SEVEN

Sarah

————————

*H*is mouth covered mine, and he spun me so my back pressed against the wall as he hauled me into his arms. I instinctively wrapped my body around his, holding tight and refusing to let go. Being with Ben allowed me to feel *alive*. Now, more than ever, I wish I could go back in time, slap myself across the face, and make myself see that Ben hadn't cheated on me. If I'd never left, we could have been together all these years, and we never would have been apart.

I never would have met Vinnie. I never would have spent months terrified of him, and what he'd do to me. I never would have lost myself, or given it all to him. I wouldn't fear for my life right now. But, then again, each road we took in life led us somewhere. Sometimes the destination was nice, sometimes it wasn't, and in this case, I might have gotten Vinnie on that road...but I'd also found a strength inside myself when I decided to walk away.

I'd grown stronger.

That mistake, that road, had made me who I was today.

Could I really regret that? Maybe, just maybe, if I had stayed here, we would have broken up, and we wouldn't be together now.

Life was crazy like that.

You never knew what you were going to get.

His hand slid down my hip and grabbed my butt, holding me in place as he thrust against me. I groaned, pressing even closer to him despite the clothes in our way. His fingers ghosted over my core, teasing me, but not fully touching.

He was everything I ever wanted. Everything I ever needed—and I needed him now. No foreplay. No gentle touches. Just him, inside of me, making me feel alive. "*Ben*. Now."

Nodding, he fumbled with his pants, undoing his belt. They hit the floor, as did his boxers. As he slid my panties out of the way, he touched me, spreading the wetness over my core. When I moaned, he did it again, and again, urging me to let go and allow him to bring me to pleasure. The faster his fingers moved, the more I writhed against him and the wall, grasping for something I knew only he could give me. When I came, stars bursting in front of my eyes, I gasped, riding his thumb as I came down from heaven.

"So fucking hot," he growled. He rolled a condom on and pressed the tip of his cock against me. His mouth melded to mine, and he thrust inside me with one smooth motion. I cried out, threading my hands through his hair as he withdrew, paused, and pushed inside me again. My stomach fisted, tightening into a ball, and I clung to him as each thrust brought me closer to that pinnacle I had just reached moments before. When I came, he was right there with me, moaning my name as he rested his forehead against mine.

We stayed there like that for an unknown amount of time. Neither of us breaking contact, or the silence. He was the first to shift away. It was too dark to see, but I felt his eyes on me. "You okay?"

I nodded. "Better than okay. Great."

He touched my cheek. "Me too."

I hesitated. "But..."

"We both know what the *but* is."

Nodding, I closed my eyes. "Don't worry, we won't tell anyone. No one will know."

"That'll only work for so long," he said, his tone low. "You know that, right?"

I sucked in a breath. "I do."

"Eventually, someone will notice. They'll see the way I look at you, or how my eyes always follow you around a room. They do, you know. I always watch you, even when I try not to." His knuckles brushed my mouth. "When you're near, I need to look at you. I can't help it."

I swallowed hard, saying nothing. Truth is, I wasn't sure what to say.

"Sarah...?"

I opened my eyes. "Yeah?"

"What we have between us...it's real. This isn't just me fucking around, or having a fling. For me? It's you. It's always been you."

We were entering dangerous territory here, but with him buried inside of me, and the darkness surrounding us, I couldn't help but be honest. "It's always been you, too, for me."

He let out a small laugh, and pressed his mouth to mine. I clung to him, happiness taking over me, and for the first time since coming back...*hope,* too. I was hopeful that this could end happy, that we could find a way out of being partners, and be together. That as partners, we could catch Vinnie, and the threat of him harming me would be over.

That I'd finally be able to *breathe* again.

There was a creak of a floorboard, a whiff of cologne, and every ounce of that hope I had went away. Because that cologne? That rise of goosebumps and fear that accompanied it?

They were all too familiar, and they belonged to only one person.

Vinnie.

Before I could even open my mouth to warn Ben, there was a sickening crunch, and his body fell lifelessly to the floor. I went down, too, as he unintentionally took me down with him since we were still entwined with one another intimately.

As we hit, I landed on my left arm painfully. I cried out, gasping for air because his lifeless body on top of mine was too much. I struggled to breathe, to push him off me, but one hand wasn't enough. I was trapped under my lover's body, who may or may not be dead.

Ben.

Sobbing, I tried to look at his face, but all I could see is the trail of blood coming out of his hair. Shut eyes, lax mouth. Struggling to breathe, I focused on his nostrils, looking for any sign of movement.

There it was. He was *breathing*.

Thank God.

Knowing he was alive, I searched the shadows for Vinnie. I didn't have to search far. He flicked the hallway light on and knelt beside me, wearing all black. His pale skin stood out against the dark clothes. His glowering eyes reflected the hate in his heart. "Hello, Sarah."

I still couldn't breathe, so I tried to push Ben off me again, but it was useless. With my arm caught under me, possibly broken, there was no way I was freeing myself. Was this how I died, trapped under Ben while he lay lifelessly on top of me? If so, at least Vinnie didn't get to touch me again.

At least I could deny him that.

"Let me guess, this is your mother's room?" He *tsk*ed, tapping something hard against the wood. Oh God, did he have a gun? "And you fucked some asshole right outside of it?"

"Go to hell," I gasped.

"Is that any way to talk to the man who could save your life right now?" he rested the tip of his gun against Ben's head. "Not to mention your mother's, and his..."

"Don't," I gasped.

He cocked his head. "Why not? He took what was mine."

The way he said that, all calm and almost emotionless, was what made him so dangerous. He wasn't like a crazy guy you'd see in a movie, who laughed manically as he killed people for fun. No, his insanity was a silent kind, the dangerous kind, and he truly thought I was still his. That what we'd once had was normal. That *he* was normal.

That's what made him such a threat.

I knew how to handle him. Knew what I needed to say to save Ben's life. Seeing the gun pressed against his temple told me something I'd already sensed but hadn't admitted to myself.

I *loved* Ben.

Always had. Always would.

I couldn't let him die for me. Couldn't lose him.

While I might not want to leave here with Vinnie, if that's what I had to do to save Ben and my mom, then I would in a second, without hesitation. So, I swallowed my hatred and said what Vinnie wanted to hear. "I'm sorry, babe."

"Yeah, sure you are." He stood, leaving me beneath Ben. The room was starting to spin now. "Let me guess? You want me to let him live?"

I nodded, trying to say yes, but failing because I was losing consciousness.

Concern colored his gaze, and he knelt beside me again. Effortlessly, he pushed Ben off me, scowling when he saw his state of undress, and my bunched-up skirt. I tried to push it down with my good hand, but he caught it. "Leave it. Show me who you really are."

I swallowed hard, tears blurring my vision. "My arm..."

He glanced at it, completely unconcerned again. "Is it broken?"

"I don't know. I...I can't move it."

He pursed his lips. "Serves you right."

His gaze went back to Ben, who was beginning to stir. His fingers twitched on the trigger, and he aimed it at his head. I sat up, cradling my hurt arm in front of me, putting myself between Ben and a bullet. "*No!*"

Vinnie scowled. "Get out of my way, or I'll shoot you, too."

"You can't do that. He's a cop."

He hesitated. "You clearly have a type."

"If you kill him, they'll hunt you down. They'll never stop. He's the captain's son," I said frantically.

Vinnie lowered the gun slightly. "I don't give a damn."

"But I do. If you kill him..." I struggled to my knees, right where he liked me best, licking my dry lips. My heart ached, and I felt like I was going to vomit. The pain...having to do this again...it was too much. "If you kill him, we can't escape."

That got his attention. "*We?*"

I glanced at Ben one last time, closed my eyes, and said the last thing I wanted to say. "Yes. If...if you help me stand, if you let him live, then I'll go with you. We'll run off together again, and I'll be yours, and no one else will ever touch me again. But we should go. Right now."

He narrowed his eyes. "Why?"

"There's a cop outside—"

He scoffed. "Not awake."

"Then when he doesn't answer, more will come." I swallowed past my aching throat, ignoring the tears rolling down my cheeks. "If we don't go soon, then we won't escape before they come for you."

He didn't even question the fact that I wanted to leave with him. Just accepted it for what it was. "You'll pay for what you've done," he promised.

I nodded, trembling. "I know."

After what felt like a lifetime of hesitation, he lowered the gun, finally taking it off Ben. Instead, he focused it on my chest, aiming for my heart. He had a better chance of hitting it when he'd held it on Ben. "Stand up."

Silently, I struggled to my feet, stumbling a bit when I straightened because I had one heel on, and one heel off. As I bent to put the other on, Vinnie caught my hair and forced me back up. I gasped, tears burning in my eyes. "Leave it off. You don't get to wear two shoes."

He dragged me along by the hair, and I got one last look at Ben before I was out the door, in his car, and we were speeding down the road. His hand was on my thigh, dangerously close to where Ben had touched me just minutes ago, and he gripped me so tight I knew I would bruise come morning. As I sat there, staring numbly out the windshield, I knew one thing without a single doubt.

If I was going to die tonight, I was going to bring Vinnie down with me.

TWENTY-EIGHT

Ben

———

"Wat the hell?" I muttered.

I opened my eyes, squinting against the pain. Why was I on the floor in a hallway, alone with my pants twisted around my thighs? I sat up slowly, blinking as I tried to clear my head. It took me a few seconds of surveying to figure shit out. Sarah's hallway. Making love against the wall. Her soft kisses.

And then...*pain*.

"Shit." I scrambled to my feet despite the darkness threatening to overcome me. "Sarah!"

No answer.

Of course, there was no fucking answer.

If someone knocked me out, there was one logical person who would have done that, and if he'd come here, she would be with him. I knew Sarah, and Vinnie had more than likely threatened my life, and her mother's, if she didn't cooperate.

Her mother.

I struggled to keep consciousness as I opened her mother's bedroom door, making sure she was unharmed. Once I ensured she was...I was going to find them, and I was going to kill him. I refused to even entertain any other outcome. Knowing that she was alone with that abusive asshole—no, I refused to go down that road. I'd find them. I'd save her.

I'd kill him.

Her mother was in bed, still tucked in and sound asleep. Creeping out, I closed the door quietly and realized I'd never pulled my pants up. As I yanked them up, I lifted my head—and locked eyes with my father. He stared at me, pale, and I froze, because he'd caught me in Sarah's house with my pants around my ankles and my dick hanging out.

I swallowed, ignoring the giant elephant in the room. "He took her."

"I figured." Dad nodded, lowering his gun. "Are you okay?"

"Yeah." I secured the button of my pants, and let go of my belt, leaving it undone. "He hit me from behind while I was distracted."

He flexed his jaw. "Obviously."

"Dad—"

"Not here." He leaned down and pushed the button on his radio. "The perp took her. Get a bolo out on a late model red Jaguar. Bollins said that's what the suspect was driving."

After he finished, I leaned against the wall, catching my equilibrium. The world was still spinning. I probably had a concussion. I didn't care. "Is he okay?"

"Yes. From what we can tell, he knocked Bollins out, and disabled the radio so he couldn't call for help. Then came in here." He squared his jaw. "To you two."

I said nothing.

"Maybe if you were doing your job—"

That broke my silence. "I *was* doing my job."

"Bullshit!" he roared, turning red in the face.

Again, I said nothing.

"Make sure someone stays with her mother. I have to go."

"You're not going anywhere," he shouted at me.

I blinked. I'd never seen him so angry.

"You broke the rules, Detective."

Shaking my head, I simply said, "I know."

"There *will* be consequences," he snarled.

"I'm the one who initiated this. It's on me, not her."

Dad scoffed. "There you go, protecting her, throwing yourself under the bus for a girl who doesn't deserve it."

I flexed my jaw. We'd shifted from our jobs, and into the personal sides of our lives. "That's not fair, Dad."

"She broke your heart once, she'll do it again."

I gritted my teeth. "We were kids back then. We're not the same people."

"Yes, you are."

Fisting my hands, I looked at him. "I love her."

He made an angry sound. "Your confusing old feelings with the connection one gets with their partner—"

"No, I'm not." I locked eyes with him. "*I love her*. I've always loved her. I always will love her. Even if she never came back, I'd still love her. Nothing will stop me. Nothing."

We stared at one another, neither of us talking.

His chest rose and fell, and I sensed he was seconds from imploding. Last time he was this angry was when I'd been ten and I'd climbed to the top of a building and perched on the edge of the roof because some kid dared me to. He'd grounded me for a year that time. I had a feeling the punishment would be much worse this time around.

"Dad..." I started.

"*Don't*." Medics came in, and they headed toward me.

Dad took a deep breath, turning his back on me. "Take him in and check him. Clearly, he's been hit too hard."

"No."

He spun on me. "Excuse me?"

"I said..." I pushed off the wall and forced myself to stand still. "*No.* I'm not going in. I'm going after Sarah."

"You are not going after Sarah. You are going to the hospital." He walked right up to me, face to face, either ignoring the fact that I was taller than him by two inches, or not giving a damn. "That's an order, Detective."

I never disobeyed an order. Never disrespected authority. Never challenged my father in the office. But this time... this time was different. Sarah was in danger, and nothing—motherfucking *nothing*—would stop me from finding her. I'd sworn to keep her safe, and I wouldn't be breaking my promise to her for a second time. "I am going after her."

With that, I started for the door.

"If you walk out that door, you're suspended from active duty," he called out, his tone final.

Freezing, I flexed my jaw. Without hesitation, I removed my badge and gun, leaving them beside the table at the door. "Then consider me suspended."

As I walked outside, I heard him let loose a string of curses, but I didn't hesitate. I headed toward my car, blinking away the fogginess. I had no idea where to start looking for her, but I'd be damned if I was going to sit around and do nothing when she was out there alone. This was on me. If I hadn't been distracted while making love to her, I could have kept her safe.

I should have kept her safe.

Leaning against my car, I pulled up our messages and checked her location. We'd decided to share our locations with one another in case something like this happened. It took forever to load, and I shook it angrily. "Come on." It loaded, and the location shown was...

Her fucking house.

"*Son of a bitch,*" I snarled, throwing the phone inside my car.

Resting my hands on the roof, I breathed heavily, the world still spinning around me. A car pulled up behind me and stopped.

A window rolled down, and Hernandez called out, "Get in."

"I'm not going to the hospital—" I started.

"Dude. I know." He revved his engine. "I have a tip on her location. I heard your dad on the radio."

"Where?" I asked, spinning on him.

He swallowed. "Get in."

"I'm going alone."

He laughed. Hard. Short. "No, you're not."

"Look, man, I'm suspended for disobeying orders. If you go with me, you'll get in trouble—"

"As if I give a damn about any of that," he snarled, angry. "I'm your best friend, asshole. You're always there for me, no matter the consequences, and I'm always there for you. He hit you, and you're probably concussed, plus you don't have a weapon. You need help, and I'm your help. Get in the fucking car."

He was right, about all of it. So, I got in, closing the door behind me. He sped away from the curb, cutting off a truck. "Word is they were spotted at a rest stop off I-5. It's a half hour from here, and the tip just came in."

I leaned against the seat, touching my head gingerly. It hurt like a bitch. "That's too much time. I was out too long. We'll never catch up."

"We've got a full tank of gas and the police on our side.

They'll be taking it slow, trying to stay under the radar, but we can go as fast as we want." As if proving his point, he turned onto the on ramp and stepped on the gas. "We'll get her."

I said nothing. I should be with her right now.

"This isn't your fault," Hernandez said, reading my mind like usual.

"Yes, it is."

He shook his head. "No—"

"When he took me down, I was inside her, telling her I was serious about us, kissing her like an idiot. I wasn't watching her back, or mine, and I wasn't doing my fucking job." I swallowed hard. "So, yes, this is my fault. If I'd kept my pants on, and my head on straight, this wouldn't have happened. I would have seen him coming from a mile away."

Hernandez stared straight ahead, cutting between two cars to get to the carpool lane. "You guys fucked?"

"Yes, we fucked." I closed my eyes. "Several times. More than that, Dad knows, and I may have cost us both our jobs."

He whistled through his teeth. "Shit."

"Yeah. Shit."

After a moment of silence, Hernandez said, "Why'd you risk it?"

"Because I love her," I said honestly. "I never stopped, but having her back here, with me, only cemented it in my brain. I love her, and if I don't find her..."

"We will." Hernandez side-eyed me. "We'll find her. No one knows you're with me, so I'll get the intel."

I swallowed. The world was starting to clear a bit. "I don't want you to get in trouble for helping me. When we get there, you can drop me off and—"

"I don't give a damn if I do, and I'm insulted that you think I would leave you on your own, without backup. We might not be partners anymore, but that doesn't change that fact that we're partners in every other sense of the word. If the roles were reversed, and I was going after the woman I loved, you'd be right there with me."

He was right. I would. "Do you have another gun?"

"Glovebox."

I pulled it out, checking the chamber and the mag. Fully loaded and clear. I set it on my lap, staring outside as we sped past moving vehicles so fast it looked like they were parked. We had to find her, as soon as possible. There was no other choice. No other option. If something bad happened to her, if he hurt one hair on her head, that was on me. It would be my fault.

How could she ever forgive me for failing her?

Hernandez's phone rang, and he hit the button on his steering wheel. "Officer Hernandez." Silence, and then: "I'm approximately fifteen minutes from there, sir." A head nod. "Yes, sir."

He hung up, and I asked: "What did he say?"

"They're at a motel frequented by hookers and drug dealers. Maybe he's getting his fix? Or he wanted a place he could pay cash without questions or records?"

"Or he couldn't wait to get his hands on her, and he's throwing logic to the wind."

"Don't think like that, man," Hernandez said, flexing his jaw. "He's probably just coming up with a plan. Maybe he's trying to sell his car or trade it for a different one. He's gotta know we're looking for him."

I said nothing.

"I've been ordered to scope it out, and then stand down to wait for backup."

I let out a hard laugh. "I'm not waiting for backup."

"I figured." Hernandez tightened his grip on the wheel. "You love her? Like, *love* her, love her?"

I nodded.

He let out a sigh. "Well, then, let's get this son of a bitch, and put an end to all this shit for the last time."

I couldn't agree more.

TWENTY-NINE

Sarah

---

*V*innie was crazy.

One hundred percent certifiably crazy.

Sometime between me leaving him, and him finding me, he'd lost it. He had this crazy cold look in his eyes that sent chills up my spine. It was almost as if losing me had pushed him over the edge—not because he loved me or anything like that...but because he'd never lost before.

Guys like Vinnie didn't know how to lose.

We sat in a dark motel room, with no lights or TV on. To be honest, I preferred it that way, because if I could see the condition of the bed he'd tied me up on, I think I'd rather he shoot me now and get it over with. This was the type of establishment that charged by the half hour, and I had no doubt if asked, they'd be all too ready to clean up an unwanted dead body or two...

For a price, of course.

Vinnie hadn't spoken a word to me since we'd gotten here. That wasn't unusual. When he was angry with me, he gave me the silent treatment as a punishment. That didn't bother me. But what came next...yeah, that hurt. After he tired of ignoring me, the real punishment would begin.

When he started talking to me, I'd be in trouble.

"I don't care, man. Just something that isn't the one I have." He paced back and forth, his burner phone on his ear. "I'd think a Jaguar could get me something nicer than a Jetta, though."

Clearly, then, he cared.

"Yeah, all right. I need it now."

Guess they settled on a suitable trade. It was smart of him to change cars, but it would have been even smarter of him to put more distance between himself and Ben. He was counting on them assuming he'd do exactly that, but the thing is, he didn't know Ben. Ben never assumed anything, and it was my hope that he continued that trend tonight, and found us before it was too late.

I'd like to say I could be my own hero, and save the day, but with my hands and feet tied so tight that I had long ago lost feeling in them...

There wasn't much hope of that happening anytime soon.

And my arm—my possibly broken one—was like an anchor weighing me down. At least without circulation in it, the throbbing had ceased. I wiggled a little bit, trying to free my feet, but it was useless.

Vinnie knew how to tie a girl down.

"Yeah, okay. If you shave a half hour off that estimate, I'll throw in some cash."

He hung up, and I stiffened. If his attention was off his car issue, there would be nothing stopping it from swinging back toward me. He walked to the window, pulling the curtain back and peering out. As he stood there, silhouetted in the moonlight, it was hard to believe that the man I'd once loved, the one who had made me laugh so hard I'd almost peed myself once, had turned into this monster who thought nothing of beating me within an inch of my life, and laying claim on me.

How could I have thought I loved him?

What happened to make him become so cold?

He dropped the curtain, eliminating any hint of light. Though I couldn't see him, I could feel his eyes on me. My heart picked up speed, and I wriggled my feet more. Again, the ties didn't budge. He was going to come for me while he had me trapped like a helpless animal in a snare.

I *hated* this.

The feeling of absolute powerlessness that he always brought out in me. It was a feeling I'd lost when I stood up to him and reported his abuse to the police, but unfortunately that feeling hadn't lasted long enough because they hadn't punished him for what he'd done.

"Sarah..." he said, his tone quiet and slow, like he had all the time in the world when we both knew he didn't. "Why did you do it?"

I swallowed, not sure what *it* he was speaking of.

Turning him in? Leaving him? Sleeping with Ben?

Back in the house, I'd had to be complacent to save Ben and my mother, but now that we were alone, and I was only fighting for my life, it was a lot harder to play the role he expected.

"Sarah."

"How did you get my number?" I asked, my throat swelling with an unnamed emotion.

He laughed. "I know people."

"And my code?" I licked my lips. "My security system?"

"I slipped in when your nurse left the door open to take the trash out." He sighed. "She should really be more careful."

I closed my eyes.

"Your turn to answer questions." He advanced on me. "Why did you do it?"

"Why are you wasting time?" I asked, my voice hollow. "You promised me months ago that the next time you saw me would be the last, so what are you waiting for?"

"Stop stalling, and answer my question."

I still didn't have an answer. "I don't know."

"Not good enough." His voice was even closer now. "Try again."

I licked my lips. They were so dry it hurt. "Go to hell—"

He backhanded me. I hadn't even seen it coming, which only made it hurt worse because I hadn't had time to brace myself for the impact. Stars swam in the darkness, and I gasped for air. He didn't usually start out with hits to the face. He saved those for last. This more volatile version of Vinnie was unknown to me. It wasn't a good feeling. "I said, *try again.*"

I bit my tongue to keep from crying out. He'd like that too much. "I'm sorry."

"Better." He sat beside me and touched my cheek with the backs of his knuckles, tracing the point of impact as if he was proud of his work. "Keep going."

"I'm sorry that I forgot—"

He ran his finger up my leg, sliding between my thighs. "You forgot what? That you were mine? That you belonged to me, no matter where you ran or who you fucked?" He slid his hand out of my skirt. "I can still smell him on you. I should have shot him for touching my property."

Something inside me snapped, and all those good intentions of trying to keep him calm, to buy myself some time so the cops could find us, flew out the window. Years of suppression and pain came flooding back, and I *refused* to do it. Refused to cower to him like nothing had changed. It had. *I* had. I wasn't the same girl he used to terrify. More than that?

I didn't *want* to be.

He was either going to kill me, or he wasn't, but I'd be damned if I died under his terms. If I was going to die, then I wanted him to know he hadn't won. He didn't scare me.

Not anymore.

"No, I'm sorry that I forgot how much of a scared little pussy you were," I said, slowly and clearly.

"I'm not scared," he said immediately. "Or a pussy."

I shrugged as best as I could while tied up. "If you say so."

He caught my chin, squeezing hard. "Admit it. Admit you're mine, and we can move on from this after your punishment. I'll even let you live."

"I'm not yours," I said defiantly, spitting in his face.

He laughed. Just laughed. He didn't even bother to wipe the spit off. "Oh, Sarah..."

"Just do it. Kill me," I demanded.

"If I kill you, I'll do it on my own time." He crawled on top of me, straddling me, and there was nothing I could do to stop him. Not with my hands and legs tied. He skimmed his hand down my neck, and over my breast. "Before that, though, you need a reminder of just how mine you are. It appears you've forgotten how this works between us. I own you. You bow to me."

"*No.*"

He stiffened. "Don't tell me no. You know I don't like it."

"Fuck you," I said, breathing heavily.

He froze. "Excuse me?"

"I said," I lifted my head, even though he couldn't see me, and glowered at him. "Fuck you, asshole."

He grabbed my hair, wrapping it around his fist. "You've gotten mouthy since I lost you."

"I've gotten lots of things. Things you could never give me."

He yanked so hard my eyes watered, and I literally felt the strands snap out of my scalp. "Shut up."

"What's wrong?" I gasped, laughing. "Don't like the truth? Can't handle it?"

"You're the one who can't handle the truth."

I laughed again, and it sounded maniacal. Not too surprising, considering the circumstances. "Oh, I know the truth. You're a scared little boy who can't keep a girl at his side without hurting her. It worked for you in the past. You terrified girls into staying until you tired of them, and told them they weren't good enough anymore. But I'm the girl who left before you finished with her. I'm the one you couldn't keep, and I've never been happier than I've been since leaving you, with Ben at my side. He doesn't have to hit me to get me to stay."

He said nothing. I think I'd stunned him.

After all, I didn't usually talk back.

I continued in a rush, taking advantage of his shock before he started hitting me. "You know, it's funny. When you walked in on us, I was about to tell him I loved him. I've always loved him. Even when I was with you, I loved him. I never loved you like I loved him—"

He closed his hands around my throat and squeezed, cutting off my words. "*Shut up!*"

I'd done it. I'd made him lose his cool.

He never did that when he was "punishing" me, so I guess it was a victory in my column. I laughed, but no sound came out, because he was literally cutting off my oxygen. Last time he'd done this, he almost killed me. This time, he just might succeed. At least my words would echo in his head for the rest of his life, and he'd know he failed to own me like he wanted. That failure would haunt him in his jail cell.

"You're mine," he spat, his saliva spraying my face.

Ben's face flashed before me, and I knew without a doubt that if I was sad of losing anything in this fight, it was him. I'd lost him all those years ago, and now we wouldn't get a chance to do it right this time. I thought about my mother, and what would happen to her, but Ben would take care of her, and so would his father. He might hate me, but he and my mother had always been close. They'd see to her care. I had to believe that.

I only wished that Ben and I had more time together. That I could have told him I loved him, and that I'd always loved him.

I wished...I wished so much.

I love you, Ben.

Vinnie squeezed even harder. "You've always been mine. You'll always be mine."

I shook my head, defying him even when I started to fade into blessed blackness.

The world faded away, and I stopped fighting unconsciousness. I tried to be happy with the small victory I'd claimed. Tried to tell myself I'd won, even though I was about to die. I *wasn't* his. I wasn't anyone's but my *own*—

and if I was going to have to go, at least I went out fighting him the only way I could. With my words. They were all I had left...

Though, he'd even managed to take those from me in the end.

THIRTY

Ben

─────────

I gestured to Hernandez with my left hand, nodding my head toward the closed door in front of me. We'd crept up on it as quickly as we dared, and so far, there seemed to be no sign of detection, but we couldn't afford to act too quickly and make mistakes.

Too much was on the line.

He nodded back, adjusting his grip on his pistol. I did the same, took a deep breath, and quietly checked the knob. It was, of course, locked.

I backed up, Glock pointed at the door, and nodded at Hernandez again. He holstered his gun, picked up his battering ram, and positioned himself at the door. Heart pounding, I took my spot to the right of him, ready to breach the doorway as soon as the coast was clear.

Hernandez mouthed: Three, two, one—*bam*.

What I saw when that door opened was something that would haunt me for the rest of my goddamned life. Vinnie had bound Sarah to the bed, and he was on top of her, straddling her, squeezing the life out of her as we watched. Rage, pure fucking rage, took over me, and almost made me forget years of police training and protocol.

But if I lost sight of the rules, if I broke them, that made me no better than him. I pointed my gun at him, locking eyes with the man who was trying to kill the woman I loved. She wasn't moving beneath him and all I could think was *I'm too late.* "Get off her, right now."

He didn't move.

I scanned the room for a weapon, any fucking excuse to take him out, but he appeared to be unarmed. Slowly, he turned his head toward me, anger burning in his eyes and his muscles bulging with pent up rage. "I should have killed you."

"Yeah, you should have." I kept my eyes on him, not letting myself worry about whether Sarah was conscious. One slip up, one mistake, and we could lose the chance we had at saving her. "Get off her, and keep your hands where I can see them."

His hands didn't leave her neck. "No."

My finger twitched on the trigger.

"I'd listen to him if I were you," Hernandez warned from behind me.

He laughed. He sounded crazy. "Why bother? We both know you're going to have to shoot me. If you put me behind bars, I'll be out in hours, just like the last time."

My finger twitched again. "Get. Off. Her."

"Why bother?" He let go of her throat and caressed her cheek as he stared down at her, ignoring the guns pointed at him. "She wouldn't admit she was mine, so I reminded her."

"She's not yours," I growled.

"Yeah, well, she's not yours anymore, either." He cocked his head. "She's not anyone's, because she's dead. I kept my promise to her."

Rage colored my vision red, and I roared as I threw myself at him. Hernandez cursed behind me, and I hit the fucker full force. We hit the ground, and struggled for dominance. As we rolled on the ground, Hernandez crept closer, his gun aimed at us as he watched with a furrowed brow. I tried to keep him down so he could get a clear shot, but Vinnie was bigger than me, and he fought with a madness that outweighed my own. In our scuffle, he got to his feet, kicked me in the ribs, and I tried to get to my own before he got to Hernandez, too.

I almost didn't see it until too late.

Vinnie found a gun and aimed it at me.

I rolled to the left as he squeezed the trigger. The boom echoed in the small room, as did the answering one from Hernandez's gun. I froze, breathing heavily, and slowly looked at Vinnie. He still stood, despite the spray of blood behind his head on the wall. He opened his mouth, blood spurting out, and then he hit the floor.

I wasted no time. Lurching to my feet, I rushed toward Sarah as Hernandez advanced on Vinnie to insure the threat had been neutralized. Sirens sounded in the background.

Our backup was here.

Too little, too late.

Crawling onto the bed, I reached for her, my hands trembling. I hesitated before touching her. She looked so... so...lifeless. "*Sarah.*"

Her skin was pale, already bruising around her eye. Her lip was bloody and split. Her eyes were shut, her mouth parted, and she held a deathly stillness to her that struck me to my very soul. I touched her skin, terrified it would feel cold to the touch, but it retained a warmth that spurred me into action. I touched her throat, searching for a pulse.

Nothing.

"No, Sar, no." I cradled her face, tears blurring my vision as pain twisted in my chest so sharp that for a second I thought I had been hit by that bullet after all. "I love you, Sarah. Don't leave me. I can't lose you again."

"Ben..." Hernandez said, his voice cracking.

All these images flashed before me. Sarah the night of our senior prom, wearing a purple dress that made her look like a princess. The tears on her face when she told me she was leaving for college, and that we weren't together anymore. The way she'd stared at me when she came back to town and found out we'd been assigned as partners. Her face after I kissed her. The tears on her cheeks as I sang to her mother. All of it was there, for me to see.

She couldn't be gone.

Couldn't be *dead.*

Not my Sarah.

We had too much to do together, her and I. Hell, I hadn't even gotten to tell her I loved her. Choking on an unshed sob, I pressed my mouth to hers, kissing her.

"I love you," I whispered against her lips.

As my mouth was on hers, she gasped for air, coughing.

I'd never been so happy to have someone cough in my face. I pulled back, eyes wide, and searched for a pulse again. It was there. Faint, but there. People rushed into the room, and chaos erupted.

I didn't pay it any mind.

My eyes were on the woman I loved. "Sarah? Can you hear me?"

Her lashes fluttered open, and she stared up at me. After a moment of silence, she opened her mouth, trying to speak, but nothing came out.

"*Shh.*" I cupped her cheeks. "It's okay. He's gone. He'll never hurt you again, I swear it."

"Let's untie her," someone said from behind me. It took me a second to realize who it was. My father. We were out of our jurisdiction, so I hadn't expected him to come personally. "I'll get her legs."

I nodded and climbed off her. Gently, we rolled her to her side as the lights flicked on. She blinked and moaned, squeezing her eyes shut against the onslaught of light. As I reached for her ties, I noticed the misshapen bend to her arm. The bruising and slight bulge hinted at a break.

My throat ached, but I swallowed past the pain. "Careful. Her arm's broken—something might be injured on her leg, too."

Dad hesitated, then touched her legs, searching for any signs of further injury. "I...I don't think so." He locked eyes with me. "Ben..."

I focused on her wrists, undoing the knots.

My hands shook too much to grip them, so it took me longer than it should have, but I finally succeeded. She gasped for air as she scanned the room. As her gaze fell on Vinnie's lifeless body, she started trembling. I quickly undid her wrists the rest of the way, and looked at the door.

Paramedics approached.

"They're almost here. They'll help you feel better."

She breathed heavily, trying to speak again. Nothing came out. I leaned closer, sensing she had something she had to say. "What?"

Her mouth moved, but nothing came out. I locked eyes with her, my chest tight and my throat even tighter. Jesus, she couldn't even speak. I almost wished the guy on the floor wasn't dead so I could kill him again.

And again. And again.

"Ben?" Hernandez said.

I blinked. "Yeah?"

"Time to get checked out for that concussion."

I shook my head, closing my hand on Sarah's. The one not currently attached to a possibly broken arm. I wasn't sure who held onto who more tightly—her or me. "No. I'm not leaving her."

"You don't have to. You can go in together."

Dad cleared his throat, then gestured to the closest paramedic. "Can you please ensure they ride in the same ambulance?"

"There's only one gurney."

"I can ride sitting up." I looked at the man. "I'm not leaving her."

"She's his partner," Hernandez said. "Come on."

The paramedic hesitated, then said, "Fine. But if you pass out, it's on you."

She clung to me, worry in her eyes. "I'm fine. They're just worrying needlessly about me. You know how hard my head is."

She tried to speak and failed...again.

"Shh. I'm here." I leaned down and kissed her forehead, even though the room spun when I did so.

"Your mom is okay," Dad added. "I left men in charge of her. She's sleeping, peacefully unaware of what happened."

Sarah sagged against the bed, closing her eyes, tears trickling down her face.

I wiped them away.

"Sir, we need to get in."

I nodded and let go of her. My hand immediately felt the loss of her skin on mine. I watched them work over her, talking amongst themselves as they loaded her up on a gurney. Behind us, a cop covered Vinnie's body with a tarp, but not before I caught Sarah staring at it.

They wheeled her out, and I started to follow. Dad caught my arm. "Son?"

I stiffened. "I know I disobeyed orders, but I don't give a damn. Fire me if you must, but don't punish Hernandez. He had nothing to do with it."

As if he sensed my words, Hernandez glanced over his shoulder at me from outside the room. He was briefing the others on what went down, more than likely.

"I wasn't going to chastise you," he said quietly. "I was going to tell you to take the week off to care for your partner."

I stared at him. "She won't be my partner much longer. I have no intention of losing her again. Not after this. Never again."

My father nodded, lowering his head. "I know. You guys are being reassigned partners because I chose to do so, not because of any wrongdoing. There will be no repercussions for you, or her. I think we all suffered enough tonight."

"Dad..."

"It's done." He shoved his hands in his pockets. "Go take care of your partner. That's an order."

I nodded, saying nothing else.

Truth be told, I wasn't sure if I could.

THIRTY-ONE

Sarah

———————

*T*opened my eyes slowly, blinking against the bright lights overhead. My head throbbed, and my arm felt torn in two. My eye swelled shut, and my throat burned. I swallowed cautiously, wincing when it hurt even more than my arm. A whimper escaped me.

There was immediate movement beside me. "I'm here," Ben said, his voice deep with exhaustion. "I'm right here, Sar."

His hand touched mine, and I turned toward him, my eyes burning with unshed tears. He stared at me, his face pale and his eyes shadowed with darkness. When I'd woken up in that motel room and seen him sitting above me, I'd tried to ask him if I was dead.

Nothing had came out.

Now, here we were, hours later in a hospital room, and I could only assume I wasn't, indeed, dead. Ben must've arrived in time to save my life. I licked my lips, and he hurried to reach for the Styrofoam cup on my bedside table.

"Doc said you could drink if you want." He pressed the straw to my lips. "So, drink if you want."

I took a cautious sip. It burned going down, but it also cooled the fire, so I took one more before sagging against the pillows again. I tried to speak, but only a croak came out.

"*Shh.* Doc said you won't be able to talk right away." He set the cup down and held my hand again. "But your voice will come back. You'll be yelling at me again in no time, don't worry."

There was so much I wanted to say.

So much I *needed* to say.

Not being able to voice those thoughts out loud was frustrating, and that familiar feeling of helplessness washed over me. It was as unwanted as it was infuriating.

His face twisted with worry, and he stood up, leaning down to kiss my head. "Don't cry. He's dead. Hernandez shot him. He saved us both. That asshole will never hurt you again."

Thank God.

"Dad knows we were together when it happened, but isn't going to punish us. He'll reassign partners, sure, but then we can be together, if you want. And if you don't want, that's okay, too." He forced a smile. "You've been through a lot, and you might want to be alone. You might not want to be with someone right now, and if that's the case, then I'll wait. I'll wait forever for you, if that's what it takes, because there's no one else I want to be with besides you."

Tears rolled down my cheeks, and I opened my mouth to speak, but again, nothing came out. I fisted my good hand in anger. I wanted to tell him how I felt.

"I know. It sucks." He forced another smile and pushed my hair behind my ear. "But you can tell me everything later. I'm not going anywhere. I'll be right here, waiting."

I gripped his wrist tight, nodding.

"I'm so sorry I wasn't able to stop him from hurting you,

and I'm so sorry I was too late to get him before he hurt you even more. If you can forgive me..." He trailed off, lowering his head. "If you can forgive me, I swear I'll make it up to you. Someway, somehow, I will."

I shook my head. He wasn't to blame. This wasn't on him, or me.

It was on *Vinnie*.

"But if there's one thing this tragedy has shown me, it's that I never want to lose you again. Whether you're at my side as my friend, my partner, my lover, or my everything..." He swallowed hard and studied my face. "...I never want to lose you again. I'll take whatever you're willing to give me, however you're willing to give it, but in the interest of full honesty, I love you. I've always loved you. I'll always love you. Nothing you say, do, or don't do will ever change that— it's just not possible to kill the kind of love I have for you."

Tears rolled down my cheeks.

"Because the love I have for you, Sar?" He reached out, smiled, and smoothed his rough, calloused hands over my skin. "It doesn't die, or crack under pressure. It just grows stronger."

I clung to his wrist even harder, nodding because the words, no matter how much I might wish otherwise, wouldn't come. Instead of trying to speak, I settled for a whisper.

One way or the other, I was going to say the only thing I needed to right now. The only thing that mattered, in the face of all this other crap. Pulling back, I looked him straight in the eyes, smiled despite my tears, and whispered, "I love you, too."

He blinked, staring at me, and then a joyous smile broke out over his perfect, charming, unforgettable face. "You do?"

I nodded, not bothering to attempt to speak again.

He laughed, cradled my face, and kissed me gently. As he pulled back, he rested his forehead on mine, and swore, "I will never lose you again. I swear to you, from this day on, to always be there for you. I'll never fail you, or make you doubt me again. I love you, Sarah."

Nodding, I squeezed his wrist and kissed him again.

I might not be able to say the pretty words back, but he knew I felt the same way. I could see it in his eyes, in his smile, in the way he watched me with that warm glow that he always had when he stared at me when he thought I wasn't looking. This time, I was looking, but he didn't care.

There was nothing to hide anymore.

Epilogue

Ben

"*A*re you sure?" I asked, smiling at the woman on the bed with me.

She nodded, smiling back. "I'm sure. She'll definitely want the purple."

"I thought she loved pink," I teased, holding up the tiny baby hat and staring at it as if I was uncertain.

Mrs. Lopez shook her head at me, clearly dismissing me for a lost cause. "She does, but every girl likes a little bit of variety in her life now and then."

"Truth," I said, still smiling. I checked the time and stood, knowing I needed to get out in the living room with Sarah, or we'd be late for work. "All right, I'll give it to her before I go, okay?"

She pouted. "Do you have to leave?"

"Yes, but start another hat. I'll be back later, and it's getting cold outside at night."

She picked up the ball of red yarn. "All right."

I bent, kissed her head, and left the room, passing Grace

as I went. We nodded at one another, and I came into the living room, scanning the room for the love of my life. She stood there, waiting by the door, two cups of coffee in her hand. Her left hand glinted in the sunlight where the engagement ring I'd put on her finger a week ago caught the sunlight.

I still couldn't believe she was going to be my wife.

There was no doubt that I was the luckiest guy alive.

"Is she good?" she asked softly.

"Yeah, she's good." I smiled at her and kissed her, the baby hat still in my hands. "How was she with you this morning?"

We took turns sitting with her every morning while the other showered and got ready for work. Then, when we were both ready, we met in the living room, and Grace took over. On weekends, we had lazy mornings where I knitted and sang to her mother, and she joined us, sometimes singing with me. I'd never been happier than I'd been these past six months, living with Sarah, in love and not afraid to show it.

Everyone teased us at the precinct, and made gagging noises when we sometimes forgot we had an audience and kissed, but we didn't give a damn.

We'd lost too much time with one another.

There wouldn't be another second wasted ever again.

"She looked like she remembered who I was for a second..." She stared off into the distance. "But then the light in her eyes went away, so I guess it was my imagination."

"I wouldn't be so sure." I hugged her, despite her full hands. "I think she gets moments of clarity, here and there."

"Yeah..." She pursed her lips. "Maybe."

"We should get going." I faked a scowl. "Your partner is waiting for you."

She rolled her eyes. "Stop being jealous."

"I can't help it. I was supposed to get him, not you."

She shrugged. "Well, he's mine, deal with it."

"Whatever." I teased her, but I was happy Hernandez was her partner now. At least I didn't have to worry about whether her new partner would have her back. Hernandez would die to keep her safe. "I guess I'm okay with Michaels."

"He's a good guy."

He was. I liked him. But he wasn't Sarah, or Hernandez. "I know." I glanced down at my hand. "Oh, yeah. We have another baby hat to donate. Purple, this time."

She stared at it, opening her mouth, then closing it.

"What? What's wrong?"

"It's nothing...it's just..." She licked her lips. "I like purple."

"I know," I said, holding it up. "But I think it's too small for you."

"I know..."

"I'll make you your own." I kissed her again. "With those fancy cables you like."

"Ben..." She set the coffees down and caught my hands. "I think we should keep it."

I frowned. "Keep it? Why?"

"Because." She rolled her eyes and sighed. "Because I'm late, dummy."

I stared at her for a second, completely confused.

"Jesus, Ben." She stomped her foot playfully. "Sometimes you're really obtuse."

"But it's only eight thirty—oh *shit*. You're *late*?"

She nodded, a smile breaking out on her face. "Yes."

I picked her up and swung her in my arms, kissing her as we whirled in a circle. She clung to me, and laughed against my mouth as I showed her just how happy that news made me. We hadn't been trying for a baby, but we hadn't exactly been *not* trying, either.

As her feet hit the floor, I hugged her even tighter, laughing. "I swear to God, woman, every time I think it's impossible to be happier than I am, you go and prove me wrong."

"I know."

She rested her hands on my chest, smiling up at me with the most beautifully perfect smile I'd ever seen in my life. I hoped our child got her smile. And her hair. And her eyes. And her passion for success. And her sense of—

"You do the same thing to me," she whispered.

"And I'll never stop." I rested my forehead on hers. "I love you, Sarah."

"I love you, too," she whispered back.

We kissed, and despite knowing she'd prove me wrong, repeatedly, I went ahead and thought it anyway: There was no way in hell I'd ever be happier than right here, right now.

I couldn't wait to be wrong again.

About the Author

Jen McLaughlin is the *New York Times* and *USA TODAY* bestselling author of sexy books with Penguin Random House. Under her pen name, Diane Alberts, she is also a *USA TODAY* bestselling author of Contemporary Romance with Entangled Publishing. Her first release as Jen McLaughlin, *Out of Line*, hit the *New York Times*, *USA TODAY* and *Wall Street Journal* lists. She was mentioned in *Forbes* alongside E. L. James as one of the breakout independent authors to dominate the bestselling lists. She is represented by Louise Fury at The Bent Agency.

Though she lives in the mountains, she really wishes she was surrounded by a hot, sunny beach with crystal-clear water. She lives in Northeast Pennsylvania with her four kids, a husband, a schnauzer mutt, and four cats. Her goal is to write so many well-crafted romance books that even a non-romance reader will know her name.

Want to know what's coming next? Sign-up for Jen's newsletter.

Connect with Jen

www.jenmclaughlin.com
jenmclaughlin6@gmail.com

Also by Jen McLaughlin

THE OUT OF LINE SERIES

Out of Line

Out of Time

Out of Mind

Fractured Lines

Blurred Lines

I'll be Home for Christmas

On the Line

THE SONS OF STEEL ROW SERIES

Dare to Run

Dare to Stay

Dare to Lie

THE MCCULLAGH INN IN MAINE SERIES

The McCullagh Inn in Maine

A Wedding in Maine

A Princess in Maine

FORBIDDEN LOVE SERIES

Bad Romance

Lust is the Thorn

SEX ON THE BEACH SERIES

Between Us

Losing Us